The Underground Allotment

Rowan Edmonds

Mudskipper Press, 2021

Paperback edition

ISBN 978 1 912226 29 0

Contents

1 Honour Amongst Thieves
2 A Solitary Vigil
3 A Private Plot
3.1 Digression: Fulham Palace
4 Night-callers
5 The Wallet
6 An Unexpected Visitor
7 Trapped!
8 Beneath the Hatch
9 Changing Identities
10 The Bridge
10.1 Digression: Putney Bridge
11 A Slap-up Meal
11.1 Digression: An Elizabethan Banquet
12 Should You Stay, or Should You Go?
13 No Lessons to be Learned from Old War Movies
14 A Day at the Football
14.1 Digression: Craven Cottage
15 The Vegetable Garden
15.1 Digression: The Poison Garden
16 Friends and Followers
17 Three-fingers Returns
18 Breakthrough
18.1 Digression: A Secret Internment
19 Rent
20 The Legacy of Alfred Wurgihurt
21 We're Only Making Plans for Alfred
22 The Dane, the Englishman, and the Refugee

Chapter One

Honour Amongst Thieves

You had never been a thief. Even in your darkest moments back home, you had never stooped so low as to steal from your neighbours. Your personal code of honour would not permit it. You don't like to think of yourself as a thief now. There must be some other term, which would better describe your activities. A recycler, perhaps? That would tie in nicely with the theme. If the reference had not been culturally inappropriate, you might have considered yourself something by way of a Robin Hood character. Stealing from the rich and giving to the poor, except, in this case, when you talk about the poor, what you really mean is you. But the fact is that you have never heard of Robin Hood; know nothing of his legend, or of his deeds. Also, your personal code of honour would not countenance the deliberate dissembling. The simple fact is that you are a thief. But you are learning to live with it.

On a scale of thieving, you like to think that your crimes would be considered fairly small fry. Petty pilfering rather than grand larceny. The kind of thing you might have been sent to the colonies for two hundred years ago, but which would not even be worth troubling the local magistrate's court over today. In Saudi, you might have lost a hand once upon a time, but you were a long way away from the Middle East now. If the history of theft was laid out on an axis, there'd be the major heists over on the left hand side—the Brink's-Mats, and the Hatton Gardens, and the Great

Train Robberies, although, once again, the references are ones outside your cultural ken—then would come the robberies with violence, the house burglaries, and the street muggings; further on would be the white-collar crimes, the tax evasions, the financial frauds, the misappropriation of funds; and then on the very far right hand side of the axis, there would be you. A virtual nonentity. An insignificant blip in the crime statistics. Nevertheless, sufficient to nag at your conscience.

You could not claim that yours was a victimless crime, but you liked to think that if you could spread the extent of your thieving over a sufficiently wide number of victims, no one individual would suffer too greatly, perhaps not even notice. That would be the ideal scenario.

Once again, you have never read the book, never heard of the character, have no similar cultural reference point from which to draw upon but, if you had, you might liken your situation to that of Peter Rabbit stealing carrots from Mr McGregor's garden. Might liken it quite favourably. Even ironically. You might also take a moment to contemplate how you have ended up, alone and penniless, such that you are forced to steal in order to survive, in this strange, unfriendly country, which holds dear in its collective public consciousness such diverse and ignoble icons as Robin Hood, the Great Train Robbery, and Peter Rabbit. You might, if you were not cold, and if you were not hungry, and if you had a mind to being philosophical, which you do not.

Yours is the mind of an engineer, both by nature and by training. You are a problem solver; adept with your hands; logical of thought. You observe a progression of unrelated events, and you find an order for them, which satisfies a need. Take your current circumstances: you have already noted that you are cold and hungry. A lesser mortal might fail to respond to these stimuli, but your background is such that you take action. The cold requires you to find some place where you can get inside and take shelter from the chill night air, but that will have to wait. The hunger requires you to remain outdoors a little longer. Remain outdoors and thieve.

It had taken you several weeks to discover the allotments. Initially, you had sought sanctuary on the harsh city streets, scavenging in the bins behind restaurants and fast food outlets for leftovers to eat. The pickings had been surprisingly rich; your newly adopted country was wealthy and their waste was correspondingly extravagant. But there had been a pecking order on the night-time city streets and, as both a newcomer and a foreigner, your position in the order could be described most flatteringly as lowly; more accurately as perilous. It was after the second beating that you had decided to move on; discover pastures new.

And there were pastures; pastures to your eyes, which had gazed for too long only on landscapes of urban desolation, poverty, war and decay. Here, in the middle of the big, noisy city was an unexpected oasis of calm. Of green. Of possibilities. There is the engineer in you speaking again. Assessing. Measuring. Weighing up those possibilities. For the first time in many months—months? Years more like—you felt an emotion, which you had thought had been lost, buried beneath the rubble of your homeland: optimism. Like a young Philip Pirrip, you even began to consider whether you might not be blessed by Great Expectations, not that you had ever heard of Philip Pirrip, of course.

While January might not be considered the peak growing season, nevertheless the bounty that could be obtained from the allotments was plentiful by your standards. Much of the produce was unfamiliar to your eyes, and it was a matter of much trial and error before you hit upon a balance of nutrients and taste, which appealed to you. It was the hard way that you discovered that Brussels sprouts are very bitter uncooked—and only marginally more palatable after cooking, in your humble opinion—and that parsnips are surprisingly tasty raw, but do not go far to slake a gnawing appetite. There were none of the citrus fruits, which you grew in your own country, no oranges and lemons, nor were there figs, pomegranates or melons, not even in the greenhouses, which maintained a temperature marginally higher than the outside freeze. But it was easy to live off cabbages and leeks and, if your diet was slightly deficient in both proteins and carbohydrates, well, beggars couldn't be choosers.

As for shelter, your choice of accommodation was almost as varied as was your menu. Most of the plots of land were accompanied by a wooden shed, ostensibly for storing tools, whilst several owners had converted their sheds into something more substantial in the way of a summerhouse, a number sporting elaborate verandas and offering accommodation over several separate rooms. Your first couple of nights in the allotments, you had spent in a traditional tool shed, the principal benefit of which being that it had been unlocked. You had cleared a space on the floor between an array of hoes and a vicious-looking scythe, spread a couple of canvas sacks; which had once stored fertiliser, on the ground beneath you and pulled a large blue square of tarpaulin over you for a sheet. You had slept fairly snugly if a little uncomfortably, benefitting from the peace of mind of knowing that you were unlikely to be disturbed by a policeman moving you on, or from a mindless drunk pissing on you when the pubs closed. However, tonight, you had loftier ambitions.

Earlier in the evening, you had chanced to notice that the door to one of the roomier summerhouse-style constructions was only latched by a simple combination padlock over a lightweight hasp. It was an invitation too good to turn down, with the potential reward of a much more spacious bedroom for the night, perhaps even some form of padded divan, which would raise you up above the level of the floor. If your luck was really in, running hot and cold on tap.

Picking locks is not a skill in your thieves' inventory, but you would defy anyone who was neither infirm nor arthritic not to have a lock of this design open inside ten minutes. In practice, it takes you fifty-two seconds, not that you are counting. The technique is very simple: listen out for the minute variations in sound when the combination wheels engage with the correct number; feel for the slight depression of the tumbler when it clicks into its corresponding cog. It is something that can be done blindfold, which is just as well since the night is starless and you have no desire to draw attention to yourself by showing an artificial light.

You slip the padlock from its hasp, loosely reattaching it once you have eased the door open a fraction. The door swings outwards with a harsh rasp, sounding unnaturally loud in the still night air. You take a pace inside, closing the door behind you, accustoming yourself to the sudden deeper darkness. Your eyes are unable to discern shape and form in the black interior. You can feel your heart racing. This initial moment of trespass is always like this. You expect the unexpected, even when rationally you know that you are alone. Nevertheless, there can still be traps for the unwary: objects to be dislodged; things left on the floor to trip over. Where, superficially the darkness is a great leveller, rendering the beautiful and the ugly alike; the rich and the poor equally indiscernible and featureless, in practice the dark provides endlessly distinct mazes, each unique with their own hazards, which have to be learned and negotiated.

You stretch out your arms, feeling tentatively ahead, like a sleepwalker; take a second step, sliding your foot forward slowly across the floor as though you are crossing a narrow walkway. Your foot finds the first obstruction; kicks against something hard. It feels like the wooden leg of a piece of furniture. Your hands explore further; discover fabric; trace the shape of a chair, quite a large chair, with upholstered arms and seat. It seems a peculiar object to find here; out of place. You hold on to the back of the chair to guide you, as you ease your way around the obstruction;

decide to take advantage of this rare opportunity for a spot of comfort, while your eyes adapt to the low light. The seat cushion sinks low under your weight. You can understand now why the chair has been moved here: some of the struts, which support the seat have collapsed; it is either waiting to be mended, or has been deliberately 'junked'; not comfortable enough for the family home; too good to be thrown away. However, by shifting yourself forward, it is still possible to sit in reasonable comfort. Your hands encounter a table top in front of you, and you lean your elbows on this, resting your head in your hands. Vision begins to return slowly, the room around you seeping into your consciousness incipiently; objects closer to you appearing first out of the darkness, sufficient to allow your brain to make a best-guess estimate of what it expects to see to fill in the most remote corners. There is a mug on the table top, in a striped pattern of colours that you cannot discern, and a small, metallic-looking dish, which is full of cigarette butts. There are a pair of gloves, grubby and worn, folded together, and next to them a pair of secateurs, in the closed position. The table is wooden, what might be described as rustic, and roughly square in shape. Beyond the far edge of the table is another chair. Superficially, it appears a matching pair of the one that you are sitting on. It is pushed back from the table, still largely cloaked in darkness. You focus your gaze upon it, staring straight ahead until, little by little, you see first the white sclerae of a pair of eyes, then the nose and then the mouth of a man sitting immediately opposite to you, staring directly back.

Chapter Two

A Solitary Vigil

He was dead, of course. It didn't require any more light to tell you that. How long? You are no doctor, despite what your mother would have liked for you. Even the full light of day would be little help for you to make an accurate diagnosis. You simply don't have the relevant knowledge. He was cold, but then so are you. But his was a different kind of cold. The coldness of finality, rather than a coldness that goes in hope of sometime being warm again. A natural death? Once again, you have no real way of knowing. He looked peaceful enough; heaven knows, you have seen enough dead bodies in your homeland that have met with a more obviously violent fate. His age? You would guess somewhere in his late sixties, but you are not very good at estimating people's ages, particularly when it comes to a race of people of whom you are not yet intimately familiar. The appearances are that he sat down in his most comfortable chair, had a fag, a cup of tea, and then just snuffed it. Massive heart attack? Sudden stroke? You simply don't know. You wonder how long he may have sat like this without being discovered? Except, something was wrong somewhere. Your logical mind is whirring into action again; the engineer's training; the joining up the dots of seemingly unconnected events. The door. Why had the summerhouse door been padlocked from the outside? There was no way that the man sitting opposite you could have performed the task. But why would anyone else lock him in? And had he been locked in alive, or was he already dead? They were questions that you had no way of answering, and your natural survival instinct warned you that you would be best served by turning your back on this scene; leave this tragic tableau behind you; relock this hut and forget that you had ever encountered this corpse sitting in its chair. After all, there was no way that you could report your discovery; it would lead to questions about yourself, which you were in no position to answer; would place you under the spotlight of official scrutiny; worse still, might even lead to you being suspected in having some hand in the unfortunate man's demise. Equally, the small mystery surrounding the locked door posed a potential secondary threat to you. Unless an unfortunate accident had occurred—and a sequence of events, which you could not logically equate to your own satisfaction—you would have to suppose that someone else other than yourself knew about the dead man in the hut, and this unknown someone was another threat to your wellbeing. Your current life, particularly the one you had begun to eke out amongst the allotments, relied on total anonymity; you could not afford to have that anonymity compromised by becoming involved in an affair, which you had no business in, practically, emotionally, morally. You don't even know why you hesitate. Your best placed course of action is perfectly plain for anyone to see. And yet you do hesitate.

Bizarre as it may sound, but the *chaise longue* might have had something to do with your hesitation. It was all part of a matching suite. The two armchairs and the *chaise longue*. Whoever the dead man had been in life, he had evidently been someone who had decided to make his summerhouse comfortable. You could picture it as his refuge. The comfy chairs, the fags, the tea. Without realising it, you had begun to build up an imaginary back story about the man, whom you only knew in reality by his corpse. Somewhere in the background, there would be a nagging wife. Or would there? Surely a nagging wife would have been out investigating his disappearance before now. Perhaps, instead, he was recently widowed, after forty years of happy marriage, leaving a home, which would once have echoed with laughter and happy memories, now a silent shell, which he could no longer bear to spend time in. The two armchairs and the *chaise longue* would have been his wife's choice; now that you could see more clearly, it was evident that the pattern of the fabric was rather swirly and flowery. They were long since passed their best, but the man would not have been able to get rid of them, not when his wife had chosen them, not coming so soon on top of her death. Here, though, in the allotments, this had always been his place; somewhere that he came to be alone; a place that he could return to without being haunted by the ghost of her presence; by the silence of her departure.

You tried the *chaise longue* for size. It still had a bit of bounce to it. On the far end of the divan, two piles of old newspapers were stacked up and, amongst them several magazines. You drew one out, holding it close to your face so that you could see the cover. It looked like something to do with gardening. Boring. You cleared the whole lot onto the floor, allowing you to be able to lie full-length on the sofa. Stretched out, your feet hung just off the far end, but it was a better alternative than the floor; offered the chance of the most comfortable night's sleep you had discovered since... since, you could almost not recall just how long. How long since you had last slept in a proper bed? Slept in a proper bed free from the fears of persecution or injury or death?

In contrast, the dead man's body held no fears for you. You are not superstitious by nature, nor are you someone susceptible to imaginary horrors. In part, this is a result of conditioning, which is nothing that you feel proud about, but it is also simple pragmatism, which is a life-lesson that has served you well. And regarding the mystery of the locked door... well, a simple chain of logic can put your mind at rest there, too. If the door was locked upon the dead man for legitimate reasons, it is unlikely that anyone will return during the night; and if the door was locked on the dead man for some clandestine reason, anyone returning was likely to want to avoid detection at least as much as you. It was with these same soothing thoughts in your head that you lay back on the *chaise longue* and fell soundly asleep.

• • •

Daylight threw a new perspective on your living quarters. The early morning sun shone directly through the summerhouse's main window, spotlighting you on the *chaise longue* as though you were a high-street window display. It also revealed aspects of the room, which you had not spotted in the darkness. Most importantly, the second door. The evening before you had taken the second door for nothing more than a recessed space in the far wall of the summerhouse, where it had showed up as just a slighter darker rectangle against a blank wall. Now, though, it offered a further opportunity, but also a potential threat. Beyond the second door lay a world of possibilities, some good, some bad. You have already stated that you are not someone blessed with an overly imaginative nature; yours is not to waste time on idle speculation, instead you move to immediate action.

The door is unlocked, and the room beyond is smaller than the one in which you had spent the night. Timber-walled, as is the entire construction, here is the more traditional 'shed'; the place where the dead man stored the tools he used on the allotment. There are no windows, and no additional doors. What had you expected? A person? That would have been one of the bad possibilities. Dead or alive, that would have been one of the bad possibilities. A toilet? That would have been a good possibility. A shower? That would have been just as welcome. Another door leading outside might have been nice, too. It might have dispelled the mystery of the padlocked front door; might have also proved to be a handy escape route. Trespassing had something in common with fire safety: it always paid to know where was your nearest emergency exit. A second door, though? It's a two-way street. What can let you out, could also let someone else in. It is just something else that would need to be guarded. On reflection, you are better off without one.

However, on closer inspection, the second room is not quite the dead-end that it first appeared. There is a small hatch in the floor, not dissimilar in appearance to a manhole cover, which looks as though it could be prized up if you had the right kind of tool for the job. Perhaps something to explore later? First must come a piss—which you do discretely in the tall shrubs, which grow immediately outside the door to the summerhouse, after first ascertaining that there is no one around to see you—and a cup of hot tea, which you brew up in the room, which you have already come to consider as 'the lounge'. Beyond where the dead man remains seated, a long sideboard runs the entire width of one wall, complete with a small metal sink, tap—cold water only—and a kettle. There is an electricity socket and, now you come to examine further, a light switch, which you flick on briefly to prove that it works, and which illuminates a bare bulb hanging from the middle of the ceiling. All the mod cons.

There is still a half cup of cold tea in the dead man's mug. You go to wash it out in order to make your own cup, but something stops you. You look at the stale liquid. A greasy residue has formed on the surface of the liquid. You sniff it experimentally. There is a faint smell that you half recognise, but which seems strangely out of place. Like the armchair; like the dead man. You place the mug undisturbed in a small recessed cupboard beneath the sink. There are several more clean mugs on a shelf in the sideboard, alongside several sealed Tupperware containers, one of which you discover contains sugar, which you leave alone, and another that contains tea bags, one of which you remove and put in your fresh mug. There is no milk, nor lemon, which you would have preferred, but you are satisfied with your lot. It is the brightest start to a new day that you have had for a long while.

• • •

A man is working in the allotment next to yours. Yours. It is funny how swiftly you have assumed a right of ownership. In your mind, you are already considering the summerhouse and its associated grounds as your possession. Somehow tenure has passed from the dead man to you, as though it had been bequeathed to you as the natural heir to his estate.

The man is taller than average height; younger than most people you would associate with owning an allotment. He seems to be working with more energy than knowledge; creating a lot of bluster without effecting any easily recognisable results. He has light-coloured hair, not blonde, but much lighter than your own, in a rather scruffy cut, and a complexion that appears more at home in the outdoors than in an office. On the whole, it is a cheerful face, you think, although some of that cheerfulness appears to come from the pleasure of manual labour; twice, now, you have chanced to glimpse him in a moment of repose, and twice the sunniness of sweat has been replaced by the winter-worn mien of worry. You observe him from the chair opposite the dead man for most of the morning. Never once does he cast a glance in your direction; shows no interest in anything beyond the immediacy of clearing dead plants and weeds from his own allotment; turning the soil with a long metal hoe; and mending a small area of meshing, which covers a patch of soil yet to reveal its crop. Even if he did glance in your direction, you feel confident that he would not be able to see you behind the glass. You have checked for yourself; while you do not have the electric bulb switched on, it requires someone to have their nose pressed practically onto the pane to penetrate the gloom of your interior. The shrubs, which grow directly outside provide a screen for your own covert observations, and the allotment plots are widely spaced offering some natural privacy. On a cold January morning, there are few people around in any case. Is it a working day? You are not sure. Or a weekend? Possibly. You had lost track of the days living on the streets; one running into the next, very much like each other, with no external routine to distinguish a Monday from a Saturday; a Wednesday from a Sunday.

The tall man on the neighbouring plot leaves at lunchtime. You watch as he packs all his tools away in his own shed—somewhat smaller than your own one—locks the door, walks away only to come back and recheck that he has locked the door, and then leaves for good. He is wearing a green quilted jacket with short sleeves, rather like a padded jerkin. It combines practical and impractical all within the same garment. More than anything else, it marks him out as a 'weekend gardener'. You can't imagine your dead man wearing a similar garment. The jacket, which lies over the back of his chair, beneath his dead body, makes no nod towards fashion or a designer label, instead is stained and grubby with the soil of the allotment; heavy and workmanlike for spending long hours toiling in the cold. The battered old gloves on the table top tell a similar story.

The afternoon passes in solitude. You spy two people briefly working on a distant allotment; two walkers on one of the paths, and that is it. By four o'clock it is beginning to get dark again. It has been a solitary vigil, but you are used to that and, all in all, you prefer your own company to that of anyone else. It had not always been the same. But there is little point on dwelling on the past. You can't change anything, much as you might want to. Your vigil reminds you of other times you have spent on sentry duty; lonely hours watching over the rooftops of your home city; the sounds and dusts of conflict rising out of the streets and buildings below; watching for an enemy, the description of which changed each day depending on political whim. On the whole, it was neither more nor less pointless than your current watch. You felt a strange sense of obligation towards the dead man; recognised that his death had permitted you this specific moment of life. Were you guarding him, or was he guarding you? Either way, you were compatriots, thrown together by circumstances outside of your control. It makes your solitude more bearable.

Chapter Three

A Private Plot

The ground in January is hard. Don't listen to anyone who tells you different. Hard for planting seeds; hard for growing vegetables; hard for burying bodies.

Three more nights had passed in the summerhouse, and your ritual had been unwavering. You had kept watch and made cups of tea by day, and you had scavenged for vegetables and slept on the *chaise longue* by night. The tall man had worked on the neighbouring allotment again the morning after you had first seen him, but he had not been back for the last two days. No one had been around to enquire about the dead man; it would appear that there was no one to care about him, either dead or alive. Otherwise, there had been nothing to disturb your routine. It was peaceful. Gazing out on the disused raspberry canes and the green mesh cloches; a pale blue January sky; the occasional contrail from a passing aeroplane; watching a robin searching for worms in the turned earth; and, as it began to get dark, a flock of starlings circling before deciding on a place to roost. Peaceful. It was a word that had been missing from your vocabulary for too long; one you feared might never return.

The only disruption to your sense of peacefulness was the smell. It had been nothing at first, but it was becoming more noticeable now. Last night, it had been hard to ignore. A sharp, putrid taint, which superimposed itself unfavourably on the pervading background damp and vegetable mulch. Now, you don't like to point an accusing finger—heaven knows, you don't smell like the proverbial bed of roses yourself; there is only so far that a strip wash and a cold tap can go when it comes to matters of personal cleanliness—but it is hard not to look towards your dead companion as the source of the offending odour. The cool January air had gone a long way to slow the natural processes of decomposition, but Time was not to be endlessly denied its bounty. Entropy dictates that all things return to chaos, and neither freezing temperatures nor spiritual persuasion were going to prevent your dead landlord from slowly returning to his component parts. It was just unfortunate that some of those component parts smelled so foul. More than your own discomfort, you realised that a stench, which would unchecked radiate beyond the summerhouse threatened to compromise your anonymity. There would be a complaint; an investigation would ensue; your squatter's rights would be exposed. It was time to act in order to forestall a potential problem.

At first, you had considered burying the dead man on someone else's allotment; there was a big mound of freshly turned earth on one of the plots close to the main gate, which would have sufficed, but you quickly realised the foolishness of this solution. Every day, you would have to live with the knowledge that he could be dug up; that any subsequent investigation would inevitably lead back to your allotment; your discovery would only be a matter of time. No. There was only one place where you could bury the dead man and be secure in the knowledge that his body remained undiscovered, and that was on his own allotment. In any case, it seemed only fitting. Earth to earth. It would have been what he would have wanted.

You had waited until after midnight before you began your primary excavations. The temperature was close to freezing, but you were used to cold nights; the winter temperature in your homeland was often similarly cold; the popular impression of a desert country is of blazing heat, but when the sun has set the temperature plummets very rapidly. It was hard work, though, and you quickly realised that to do a proper job was going to take longer than the single night that you had allotted. There was another problem, too. No matter how you try to disguise it, a six-foot by two-foot trench looks remarkably like a grave, in anyone's money. In an attempt to conceal your activity, you expanded the scale of your digging; turning over the soil in a wider plot all around your main trench, although to a lesser depth. Superficially, it looked better; not so immediately suggestive. After a couple of hours of steady spadework, you were all in. Weeks of poor food had not been kind to your resources of stamina. In the past, you would have toiled in the heat of the day without need to pause; now, you found yourself shaking with exertion and sweating despite the cold. You were getting old; your body was no longer as fit as it once was. You needed to sleep, if you were to continue your vigil by day. Your last tasks were to even out the excavated soil, so that it did not appear such an obvious heap, and to pull a large tarpaulin over the entire area, to hide it from potential prying eyes. You estimated that you had dug down to a depth of about two feet. It was not far enough. Not by a long way.

Digression Three.One
Fulham Palace

Dig two feet down in most parts of the city, and you hit something solid. Concrete, clay, chalk, stones. The soil of the city is nothing more than a thin veneer of the countryside laid on top of the artificial foundations of the urban metropolis. Except not in the allotments.

The allotments are situated on ground that had once formed part of the gardens of Fulham Palace. Tucked away, in a discrete corner by the main gate, is an informative signboard, which had educated you all about them. It is a fascinating account; told you much about the history of your newly adopted land; began to give you an insight into the psychology of the strange people who maintain Robin Hood and the Great Train Robbery and Peter Rabbit in their collective consciousness.

The site has been home to Roman colonisers, Saxon settlers and Viking invaders. Its position close to the River Thames made it an important meeting point for travellers, traders and pilgrims; the tourists of their day. The history of Fulham Palace as it currently stands dates back to the mid-13th Century, but the land had been owned by the Bishops of London for over 500 years before that. Deep, fertile, rich loam, suitable for bishops to garden; the same thick earth, which you had discovered was ideal for burying bodies.

The early Bishops of London used Fulham Palace as a summer retreat, somewhere to escape the grime and the dirt and the smells and the people in the crowded city centre; you liked to think that you were carrying on the same proud ecclesiastical tradition. Kings and Queens have been guests within the Palace grounds, and Queen Elizabeth I presided over a lavish banquet in the Palace in 1601.

Throughout the ages, various bishops proved themselves to be enthusiastic gardeners, and the fortunes of the Palace gardens reflected the respective green fingeredness of the resident incumbent. Bishop Henry Compton was a recognised botanist and populated the gardens with exotic plants gathered from the rapidly expanding British colonies; Bishop John Robinson was altogether more pragmatic—or gluttonous—and tended to plant only those crops, which could be served at his table; whilst Bishop Richard Terrick created the walled garden, which still exists today.

It was during the First World War that a portion of the Palace gardens was requisitioned to grow crops for the population of London, and the current-day allotments were born. And it is in a small corner of the same Palace gardens that a refugee from a distant land now calls his home.

• • •

The following night saw you back at the same task at the same time, but an icy, thin drizzle had set in, which was dispiriting and had the effect of making the soil cloying and even harder to dig. It required a third night's labour before you had dug a pit sufficiently deep for your purposes, and were then faced with the tricky problem of transporting the body to the hole.

The dead man would never have been described as a 'looker' when he was alive, and death had done nothing to add to his appearance, nevertheless you had become accustomed to him, sitting silently in his chair; apart from his smell, he had been an easy flatmate, undemanding, and you experienced a tinge of sadness as you gazed upon his vacant features for a final time. Once, his eyes might have sparkled with amusement, where now they stared blankly, the pupils rolled slightly back into the head, and a mouth, which might have occasionally crinkled telling a wry anecdote, was now just a gaping yawn. The nose remained unchanged; most probably had always been his most prominent feature, bulbous and, in recent years, criss-crossed by a thin tube-map of broken capillaries.

You moved the table slightly, to give yourself a bit of working space, and cleared a passage to the door. For the first time, you could see the entire body and legs of the man, where before they had been largely concealed beneath the table. He was taller than you realised; which also gave him the effect of looking thinner, particularly in the strange shadow-light of the moonlit window. You couldn't make an accurate guess as to his weight, but you knew that he was not going to be easy to shift. You made one or two half-hearted, experimental holds around his torso, only succeeding in causing his arms to swing wildly like gangling pendulums, and releasing several noxious pent-up farts from the folds of his clothes. You stepped back to consider the matter; set your engineer's mind to the task.

First job: remove his shoes. This had little to do with reducing the overall weight of the corpse, and more to do with the fact that you appeared to share a shoe size with the dead man, and his lace-up brown brogues were in rather better repair than your street-weary white trainers. They did not seem like gardening shoes, but then what did you know? You had not thought that your neighbour's green padded jacket was particularly suitable gardening attire either. You wondered if there were any other clothes that you could make use of before you buried them for good but, even during the brief few moments you had already spent grappling with the corpse, you had noticed several distinctly unsavoury stains seeping through the garments, and so you decided that it was only proper than your dead companion be buried complete in all his finery.

The effects of rigor mortis had long since worn off the body, and the muscles of the corpse had relaxed again making it sag like a puppet cut of its strings. If you could only get your head underneath its armpit, you thought that you might be able to swing the dead weight around, supported by your shoulders and back in a fireman's lift. Standing and staring at the problem was not going to make it any easier; once again, it was a time for decisive action. You take a step back from the dead man, and then turning quickly as though to catch him by surprise, you put your head down, at the same time lifting up his nearest arm and using this useless limb as a lever from which to transfer the weight of the main body up and over your shoulder. You almost stagger and fall but, by shifting your feet you retain your centre of balance and, little by little, manoeuvring the dead body all the time, you manage to stand up and take a tottering step towards the door. Another big shrug of your shoulders and you have the weight distributed evenly, with the man's long legs hanging down your back, and his head lolling uncomfortably close to your face. At one point, you think that you feel his distended tongue lick the side of your neck, and you almost retch at the smell of his body in so close proximity to your own, but three confident strides take you to the door, and one more out of the summerhouse, where the cold night air provides a reviving tonic. Your footsteps fall unnaturally deeply into the freshly turned soil, and you realise that you are walking with the tread of a man twice your normal weight. You sense, rather than see, something fall from the dead man, landing somewhere behind you, but you are not able to look back; if you falter in your stride, you know that you will not have the momentum to start up again. Six more paces, and you are standing in front of the makeshift grave. In your imagination, you had planned to say some pertinent and spiritual words at this point, but mundane fatigue takes precedence and, instead, you simply swing yourself around in an arc, letting go of your heavy cargo such that it is propelled a short distance through the air, to drop half-in, half-out of your prepared pit. It is only the matter of a few seconds' extra work for you to edge the body over the side of the chasm, where it folds up into an awkward shape at the bottom of the hole. You straighten up, breathing heavily, shaking out your aching muscles, exhausted both from physical exertion and nervous tension. You look down into the pit. It is not the end that you would have chosen for your erstwhile companion, but you are not overly sentimental, and you are pragmatic enough to recognise that he no longer cares one way or the other.

Your night's work is not over, though. Far from it. Now you must fill in the trench, and this is not a job that can be spread leisurely over three nights; it must be completed before daybreak. Thankfully, the task of filling the hole is much quicker and easier than that of digging it, and you find yourself reinvigorated with the prospect of a good job almost completed. It is not long before you are on your hands and knees, levelling out the surface of the disturbed earth, attempting to make it appear like nothing more than a newly-turned strip for planting cabbages. To complete the illusion, you drag two green-netting cloches from where they have been folded up and stowed beside the summerhouse, and erect them over the freshly-dug ground. They look rather like a forensic tent laid out by a scene-of-crime officer, but you are sure that it is only your guilty conscience that is making the analogy. The last job for the night is to return your spade to its rightful place in the shed, and then you are done.

Chapter Four

Night-callers

A policeman patrols the allotments twice each night. Once at 10PM and then again shortly after 2AM. You have got quite used to his routine. He enters by the main entrance gate on Bishop's Avenue and he leaves by the delivery entrance on the north side of the Fulham Palace car park. The distance between the two points is about 250 metres and it takes him an average of five minutes to do this patrol. This includes the 45 seconds he spends having a piss in the corner of allotment number 72. It is the same place each night. The owner of the allotment in question must be left baffled as to why his sprouting broccoli seem so blighted. It is only the hardiest of plants, which can thrive in such an ericaceous soil. You would suggest a nice heather.

A 'copper'. It is a term that you had heard during the time you had been living on the streets. "Look out, there's a copper coming." It had been a frequent nightly reveille. Or: "Scarper. Coppers." The copper who patrols the allotments is no bother to you. Your summerhouse is not on his beat. Nevertheless, you are careful to coordinate your vegetable gathering activities to times when he is not due to be on watch.

He is not the only night-time visitor.

You have urban foxes. One very manky individual, who keeps to himself, always fleeing as soon as he picks up your taint, and who limps badly on a deformed back leg, and a pair of younger cubs, who jump and engage in play fights with one another, and who do not seem bothered by your presence. There may well be others. Sometimes, if you are still awake during the early hours of the morning, when the allotments are at their darkest, you hear their banshee-like wails, like the screams of terrified infants trapped under the rubble of toppled apartments—be under no illusion, it is an analogy you make from experience, not from some kind of macabre poetic licence.

Once you spotted a courting couple climb the perimeter wall, the ardour of lust fuelling their athleticism and, on several occasions, an odd vagrant has tentatively looked in, but never to stay long, not being blessed with either your wit or ingenuity to see the potential of the locality.

You have heard several tawny owls—a rather tuneless whistle rather than the iconic 'twit-twoo'—but you have yet to see one; and you have seen several bats, flitting swiftly as dark shadows against the night clouds.

The most common visitors are cats. You have identified three as regulars. There is a tortoise-shell with one eye, who you have christened, perhaps unkindly, 'Blink'; there is a large black cat who spits and gets into pretend fights with itself; and there is a slender white cat, who is your least favourite, mainly because she has adopted a corner of your allotment as her own personal litter tray and, despite her 'butter-wouldn't-melt' appearance, is capable of producing the most gut-renching, foetid faeces. Nevertheless, it is this smelly-shitting ghost-face who discovers the wallet.

Chapter Five

The Wallet

At first, you thought it must have been a small rodent. You had never seen the white cat catch anything before; believed her to be more a pampered, three-tinned-meals-a-day, rather than a catch-it-fresh-yourself kind of cat, but that was your first impression. It was only as you moved closer, and the cat retreated, leaving its find behind, that you discovered it was a wallet. You recalled now your impression of something dropping from the dead man's body as you had unceremoniously conveyed him to his final resting place. It must have slipped from his trouser pocket or, more likely, perhaps from an inside pocket in his jacket. You picked it up, wiping off a few spots of accumulated dirt from the leather, automatically weighing its quality in the palm of your hand. It felt quite thin; the comforting thinness of familiarity.

Back inside the lounge, the door shut, your eyes accustomed to the darkness, you began to pick through the contents of the wallet. You spread them out on the table top, taking out one item at a time, treating each piece with the sanctity of a sacred relic. By rights, this object should have been buried alongside its owner. It's possession made you feel as though you were nothing better than a grave-robber, although, to ease your conscience, you tried to spin yourself more in the 'guise of a Howard Carter than that of a Burke and Hare.

First of all, there were the banknotes. These were still relative strangers to you, although you could read the denominations. On two occasions, while you had been sleeping rough on the streets, you had had a banknote cross your palms; once a 'fiver' from a 'Kindly of Kensington', doing her good deed of the day, and once a 'twenty' from a 'Wideboy of Wapping', pissed as a newt, at pubs' closing time. Mostly, though, you had only accumulated a wealth of small change: one pence pieces, twos, fives, tens, twenties, fifties, a pound coin, very occasionally a two-pound coin; sometimes a half-pence piece, which you quickly discovered had long since gone out of circulation. Small change, which was spent as quickly as it was accumulated; which had disappeared long before it ever succeeded in becoming a weight troublesome enough to disturb the lining of your trouser pockets. This time you counted out seven notes, all identical 'tenners', plastic and shiny. Seventy pounds. The pound was the same unit of currency as in your own country, but you knew that seventy pounds in Britain was worth considerably more than the equivalent amount in your own currency; about 700 times and counting. The twenty pounds in Wapping had seemed like a windfall; this was an extravagance beyond your wildest dreams. And yet it also felt like theft. Instinctively, you recognised that a wallet full of money propelled you into a higher league of criminality on your graph of thieves than did a handful of Brussel sprouts. When you had devised your scale, you had never even considered the prospect of grave robbing. You were moving away from petty pilfering and edging towards street mugging territory. It was a slippery slope.

Nevertheless, you collated the seven 'tenner's into a neat bundle, folded them once, and stuck the small wad into the back pocket of your trousers.

There was a credit card, kept separate from the cash by a small leather pocket inside the wallet. For the first time, you are given the name of your dead landlord: Alfred Wright. You say the name out loud. The surname is a sound unfamiliar to you. Wurgihurt.

"Alfred Wurgihurt."

You quite like it. You can imagine it being the dead man's name. You say it again, more confidently this time:

"Alfred Wurgihurt."

You can imagine it being your name.

Tucked away, almost out of sight, in the same little pocket as the credit card, is a small slip of paper, folded into quarters. Written on the slip are four numbers. 4627. A four-digit PIN. It would appear that Alfred Wurgihurt had not altogether trusted his memory. You refold the paper, and replace it with the credit card in the wallet.

In the large pocket of the wallet where you had found the banknotes, there are a couple of shop receipts, slightly crumpled, hastily stowed. There is also a supermarket loyalty card, and a book of twelve second-class stamps, with only two remaining. The receipts fill in a little background detail to the dead man's life; seem to corroborate that some of the guesses you have made about his circumstances might not be so far from the truth. One of the receipts is from the same supermarket as the loyalty card: most of the purchases appear to be microwaveable ready-meals for one, and four-packs of cheap lager. The other receipt is from a newsagent for cigarettes.

You are surprised not to come across any photographs in the dead man's wallet; you had always carried photographs of your own loved ones in your own wallet; when you had owned a wallet of your own; when you had had some loved ones. There are no photographs of the dead man's recently deceased wife; no photographs of any children. Had they been a childless couple? Or perhaps there is a solitary child, grown up now, a son, who lives abroad, in Australia, or Canada, where he moved for his job, married, with children of his own, doing very nicely. Doing so nicely that he wouldn't have any need for any of his dead father's money; you didn't like to think that you might be doing anyone out of their inheritance. Doing so nicely that he didn't have any need for a father, period.

You put the items back in the wallet, and place the wallet in the top drawer of the sideboard. There, it appears less like theft and more like 'safekeeping'.

The lace-up brown brogues sit neatly together beneath the table, almost in the exact same position as when they had been filled by the feet of the dead man. The possession of them does not feel like a theft in the same way that the wallet does. Here, it is more a case of recycling; it would be more a crime to have let them go to waste, buried beneath the earth. In your mind, they fall under the category of an *objet trouvé.* The difficulty you now have is in simply disturbing them, because to move them, even by a small fraction, will upset the connection that they maintain with their past owner and, with it, their power as a piece of art. You decide to let them remain in their place as a memorial to Alfred Wurgihurt. You had not been able to erect any kind of grave marker above the actual spot where he is now buried, but his shoes will stand testimony that he is never forgotten.

Chapter Six

An Unexpected Visitor

You have overslept. It is unusual for you. The combination of your exertions of the previous night and the lateness of the hour when you finally laid down on the *chaise longue* have resulted in this lapse into tardiness.

There is the sound of voices from outside. The noise stirs you to instant alertness. You cross to the window, keeping low, peer above the sill, making sure that you remain in the shadows. The tall man with the green jacket is once again tending his allotment. He has a long gardening fork in his hands, but he is currently leaning on it, not using it. Beside him, standing with his back to you is another man. A man you have not seen before. An older man, judging by his stance and his clothes. He is wearing a flat, checked cap, and untidy tufts of white hair stick out from beneath it. You can see him gesticulating behind him, pointing as though in the direction of your summerhouse. You feel a cold chill of fear sweep over your body. For so long, you have grown accustomed to anonymity; this close proximity of people seems more like a hazard than anything welcoming. You edge away from the window and move closer to the door. By easing the door open a fraction, allowing the hasp to unbuckle to the limit of its hinge, you are able to create a small crack through which it is possible to eavesdrop on the conversation taking place outside. You hear the voice of the tall man speaking first.

"Alf? I don't know him, I'm afraid."

There is more pointing towards you, followed by:

"Old Alf. You must know. His is the allotment next to yours."

The tall man looks towards you. You feel as though his eyes must spot you; see you cowering behind the door; sneaking a glimpse through the thin gap, but his look is completely disinterested; taking in no more than the general scene; not looking at the specifics of the picture.

"'Fraid not. You see, I'm only looking after things here for my mother. It's her allotment, really. But she's had to go into a care home recently. We'll have to give it up altogether, but I thought I'd spend a couple of weekends tidying things up before we hand it back to the site managers."

"And you've not seen anyone working over there?"

"No one. But, like I say, I'm only here weekends. Are you a friend of… Alf, is it?"

"Friend? Yes. I suppose you could say that."

"Well, I hope you find him."

"Thanks. I might just have a look around."

"Good idea. Well, Best of British."

"What?"

"Good luck."

"Oh, right. Yes."

The older man turns, and you instinctively spring away from your viewing post at the crack in the door, before edging back again to continue observing. You have watched and waited like this at times in your past; looked out across the ruined rooftops of your home city; kept watch, observing without being seen through shell holes in blasted building's masonry; spied across the shattered streets to where an unseen enemy might be watching back, or existing only in your fears.

The older man is definitely real. But a threat? You are not yet sure. He is slightly stooped, his eyes constantly cast upon the ground ahead of him, as though unsure of his next footfall. His face is in shadow beneath his cap, but you can see that it is heavily lined, and browned in a way that suggests a life lead largely out of doors. You are put in mind of fishermen in your own country; perhaps this is what genuine gardeners look like in this one? He has crossed from your neighbour's allotment to stand at the threshold of your own. The freshly dug earth appears to have attracted his attention. You can see the lines deepen on his forehead as though in thought or surprise. He makes a tentative kick towards one of your newly placed cloches, muttering something under his breath, which you are unable to hear. He briefly turns back towards your tall neighbour as though to ask a question; checks himself seeing that that man has resumed his own work; realising that he is looking in the wrong direction for the answer to his unvoiced question. For a moment, he looks directly towards the summerhouse; directly towards you. Despite the weather-beaten decrepity of his face, the eyes that stare from it are lively and alert. Unlike the tall man, whose gaze was abstracted and unfocused, the older man's attention is sniper-sharp. You feel as though he is taking in every minute detail of the scene before him;

examining the summerhouse for the tiniest sign of change. You raise your assessment of his level of threat one notch higher.

There is an element of caution in his approach though. You feel puzzled; this is not the easy visitation of one old friend hunting out another; there is something circumspect about his manner; almost covert. You are torn between wanting to continue to observe, and wanting to hide and seek cover. However, you have left it too late to leave the summerhouse; there is no possible way to get out through the door without being spotted. Even if you ran and evaded capture, it would inevitably lead to your sanctuary being compromised, and that was the very last thing that you wanted. You had scarcely had the chance to sit back, relax and revel in the pleasure of home ownership; you were not yet ready to have that hard-found security cruelly snatched away from you so soon.

However, it is beginning to become apparent to you that the elderly invader is not going to be content with a casual kick of your cloches and a perfunctory sweep of the perimeter of your territory; he is hell-bent on invasion, and there is little that you can do to repel him. His approach is more purposeful now; the older man is beginning to walk directly towards where you continue to cower behind the summerhouse's front door. You can count down the seconds before he will be standing directly beside you; six, five; can visualise the paces between him and his target. Four, three. Stay or withdraw? Two, one. You have only seconds to make a decision.

Discretion is the better part of valour. You have no cultural affiliation with the phrase; no close reading of Shakespeare, although you had been obliged to read a version in translation at high school; no blood line that might be expected to link you back to Henry IV; nevertheless, you instinctively recognise that to retreat is your most sensible option given a limited range of alternatives. There is the logic of the mind of the engineer at work again but, also, the military strategist: you had been involved in enough conflicts to realise that nothing is achieved by giving up your life cheaply; you needed no knowledge of either Demosthenes or Goldsmith to recognise that it was better to live to fight again another day, rather than to sacrifice yourself unnecessarily against unfavourable odds.

The lounge area of the summerhouse offered few places where it would be possible to hide. There was room to squeeze either under the table or under the *chaise longue*, but neither would confound even the most basic scrutiny. The sideboard offered no opportunities; your only hope lay in the shed area, trusting that the unwelcome invader would not have reason to penetrate beyond the first room.

Outside, you could hear a quiet footfall almost at the doorstep. There is a slightly raised concrete platform, which skirts the entire property, and you could visualise the newcomer's first step onto this boundary terrace. Shortly, his sun-wrinkled face would be pressed at the glass of the window, attempting to peer inside before making the inevitable step to trying the door. There was no time to lose.

You open the door to the shed, step inside, and close it behind you in one swift movement. There is a sensation of the outside world being blocked off from you here, but you are confident that you will still be able to pick up sounds of the man if he actually enters the summerhouse. There are even fewer places of concealment open to you than in the lounge. You wish you had previously taken the time to investigate the hatch in the floor, but it is too late for that now; you have no tool immediately at hand with which to prize it up. You can do nothing more than stand behind the door, and hope for the best.

Seconds pass. Long seconds. Long seconds turning into minutes. Nothing happens. There are no sounds from the adjoining room; no reason to believe that the front door has been opened; no sense of the presence of the older man. You have heard of the British reputation for politeness; you wonder whether it is a cultural step too far for the other man to actually enter someone else's property without having received an express invitation. An Englishman's home is his castle: it is not just a well-used phrase, but a legal precept.

"Alf."

The voice is so close that it makes you jump. The older man has not only entered the summerhouse, but sounds as though he is standing directly behind the door next to you. Now that you reattune your hearing, you can hear him clearly; hear him moving around; hear him breathing. Like a form of synesthesia, you can visualise his actions in the adjoining room by the sound of his movements. You hear him scraping the chair—the one closest to the door—hear him open the sideboard cupboard—the topmost one, nearest to the window—hear him move the dead man's shoes—why move the shoes, the inviolate shoes, of all things? The sounds are subtler now, and you press your ear closer to the wood of the internal door, attempting to decipher the minutest alterations of pitch and tone. The older man is examining the other chair now; the one where the dead man had sat; examining it good and hard, longer than is strictly necessary. You can hear him picking up things on the sideboard. A mug? The Tupperware caddy containing tea? His breathing sounds harsh and wheezy; there is a catch on every third breath, as though he is having to draw in extra oxygen into his lungs. You can hear his footsteps on the bare wooden floorboards of the summerhouse; hear a small creak and see the minutest rise of a floorboard beside you as the man beyond the door transfers his weight to the other end of the old wooden plank. Any second now and the door will be flung open and you will be discovered.

Horror movie clichés are the same the world over; you've seen the scenario plenty of times before; already know what is going to happen next and begin to anticipate. As if in slow motion, the handle of the door begins to turn. It is one of those round, beehive-style knobs, rather than an up-down lever-style one, and you can see the concentric rings of the knob slowly rotate. You feel like you are in a movie; can picture yourself, as a kid again, thrilled, in the front row of the small cinema theatre, sitting forward in thrilled anticipation of what is going to happen next on the big screen. It makes it easier, somehow, removing yourself from being the centre of the action; repositioning to be a mere onlooker, one amongst many, no one special, anonymous once again.

The door is opened cautiously, and you find the space you inhabit behind it squeezed and reduced, making you involuntarily suck in your stomach and hold your breath, as though those actions will diminish your physical frame proportionate to the shrinking gap.

"Alf?"

The older man's hand is on the doorframe; you can see his fingers furled around the outside edge, close to the lock rail. They are clearly a smoker's fingers, the tips stained brown with nicotine. You can imagine him sitting at the chair by the window in the summerhouse, the dead man sitting opposite him, both talking, both smoking, the pile of stubbed out cigarette butts in the dish on the table rising higher. One of the older man's fingers is shorter than the others. The little finger on his right hand is missing the distal phalanx. You wonder if it had been a gardening accident?

"Alf?"

The man makes no move to enter the shed. It is evident from his position at the doorway and from his repeated calls that the object of his search is not there. Slowly, the stained fingers unwind from the edge of the door frame, like a spider retreating back into the centre of its web, and disappear from sight; slower still, the door is pulled back closed, shutting with a faint click. There is the creak of the loose floorboard again, quiet footsteps, and then nothing. You are alone.

Chapter Seven

Trapped!

The sugar container is missing. You have checked several times, but there can be no doubt about it. The tea container is still in the same position, but the sugar one has gone. You have opened all the drawers of the sideboard, but it is not in any of them; there is nowhere else that it could be. The only explanation is that the older man has taken it. It seems like a strange thing to take away. Except… perhaps that was the purpose of his visit all along? To borrow some sugar from a fellow allotment owner? Momentarily, it raises the spectre that he may soon come back to return the item, but only momentarily. His entire approach had been too guarded merely for it to be a companionable neighbour on the cadge. There was something wrong somewhere. Instinctively, you check the dead man's mug; it still remains where you had first placed it, unwashed, in the small recessed cupboard beneath the sink. Well, he had not found that. The loss of the sugar is of no consequence: you never take it in your own tea.

The shoes were something else, though. Their disturbance felt like a desecration. They had not been removed, but they had been taken from their neat position beneath the table, and idly kicked more towards the sideboard so that one now lay on its side; no longer a memorial, merely unloved castoffs. The act of vandalism had destroyed the integrity of your shrine and, with it, the last spiritual link with the dead man disappeared too. Now you were on your own.

You glance through the window. There is no sign of the older man. The tall man is still working on the neighbouring allotment. You are surprised to see that the sun has come out and, although the temperature outside must still be scarcely above freezing, the tall man is sweating from the exertion of his work. He has removed his padded green gilet and left it hanging over the handle of a spade, which stands upright, stuck into the recently turned soil, giving the ensemble something of the appearance of an upper-class scarecrow, or a minimalist shop window display in the King's Road. You pull out the dead man's chair and sit down. It affords a better view outside from where you can see and yet not be seen. It is strangely therapeutic watching the tall man work; it relaxes your body; allows your muscles to rest. You had not realised quite what an effect the strain of having to conceal yourself behind the door of the shed had had on your body. Both your arms and your legs are shaking slightly from the release of tension; you can still feel your jaw clamped unnaturally tight; your teeth grinding against one another in a way that you are powerless to control. It is a relief to sit down; your whole body feels uncharacteristically weak; your mind without focus. The tall man has finished his work—a large pile of uprooted serpent-like weeds and spiky stubs of pruned shrubs evidence of his efforts—and is now sitting astride the corner of an upturned wheelbarrow, his figure largely turned away from you, drinking from a brilliant-red Thermos flask. When he replaces the silver top of the flask, the sunlight reflects off the shiny metallic surface and dazzles like a laser beam.

You guess that it must be close to midday. The tall man is making moves to pack up; you are getting used to his routine; you wonder if he has other commitments in the afternoon; a family of his own to spend time with? He locks his shed and walks a few steps away; returns; checks that the shed is definitely locked, then leaves for good. It is like a nervous tick for him. You are glad to see him leave; you are desperate for a piss—have been for some time—and his departure allows you the opportunity to slip outside and relieve yourself in your usual spot. You take a last look through the window to make sure that the coast is clear, and then move to the front door, ready to leave.

The door won't open. At first you push it gently, easing it forward cautiously in the way that you do when you normally leave the summerhouse then, when it does not budge, you push harder. Still, it resists any attempts to open. Immediately, you recognise the problem. It is locked. From the outside. Upon leaving, the older man has refastened the padlock to the hasp on the outside of the door, effectively trapping you inside. You could easily break your way out by brute force several well aimed kicks would be sufficient to splinter and split the thin wood panels—but the violence and noise might attraction attention, and you would be left with a damaged door, which you are not in a position to quickly fix and which could not fail to initiate some kind of investigation. A different solution is required.

Once again, your mind goes back to the hatch in the floor of the second room. It does not provide an obvious means of immediate escape, but it does continue to nag at you as being a part of your domain that you have yet to fully explore. As evidenced by the arrival of the older man, some kind of secondary exit from the summerhouse might prove extremely useful, and the hatch in the floor offers possibilities, if nothing more definite. However, at the moment, the need to piss is stronger than the need to explore; you need a means to get out, and quick.

The window offers no solution. It is a sealed framed unit, not intended to be opened. You return to the door. It is the only practical answer. When it is required, your engineer's mind clicks smoothly into gear. It was the same in your homeland; the same when you were trapped there; where others might have panicked, instead you looked to practical solutions; thought only in terms of statistics and percentages. How much oxygen was left to you? How many tonnes of rubble were piled above you? How long would it take before the rescuers reached you? Here, the circumstances are less life and death; the calculations altogether more mundane.

All that you require is a screwdriver; Phillips head for preference, but you are confident that you can make do with any variety. You return to the shed. There is a large, metal toolbox on the floor in the far corner; so far, you have not had any reason to properly examine it, but you are confident that the dead man was sufficiently adept at do-it-yourself that he would have maintained a well-ordered, well-equipped set of tools. You have come to think of Alfred Wurgihurt as something of your guardian angel, and you do not expect him to let you down now, in your hour of need.

True to expectation, the very screwdriver lies close to the top of the tool box. You can almost feel Alfred Wurgihurt's hand passing it over to you:

"Here you go, son."

It is the matter of only a few seconds' work for you to loosen the screws, which fasten the hinges of the front door to the door frame. Supporting the door's weight, you allow it to settle slowly, preventing it from splitting the wood where the hasp connects to the middle rail. Slowly, you swing the door outwards, a mirror-image of its normal function. Your freedom arrives with a blast of cold air. It only exacerbates the desire to pee. As far as you can tell, no one has witnessed your emergence; there is no one else around to observe you; your blessed shrub awaits you.

Relieved, in all respects, you push in the combination for the padlock, and unfasten it from the hasp. You will have to look into some other means for securing the front door; one that still operates when you are inside. You look around you. It is a beautiful January day. Cold, but sunny. A pale, blue sky, almost cloudless, and only the slightest breeze. You remember how the tall man had worked up such a sweat earlier, working in these conditions. You look across to his allotment. The King's Road scarecrow continues to sway bleakly; in his departure, the tall man has forgotten to take his green quilted jacket; it remains hanging, where he left it, this month's essential fashion item for the self-respecting spade about town.

Theft, or another *objet trouvé*? The two states are beginning to blur and merge. There is no one to see you; no witnesses if this is a crime; no spectators if this is an exhibition. You walk over to your cloches; over the recently turned earth beneath which the dead man is buried; cross the narrow hard-earth path, which separates your allotment from your neighbour, and remove the green jacket from the handle of the spade in one confident movement of ownership. At the same moment, a loud cheer rings out behind you. It is the sound of multiple voices, united in expression. You spin around, startled, guilty; searching for the source of the noise. The sound is repeated, slightly quieter now, and gradually dies away into a general background murmur competing with the sound of a loudspeaker announcement. You knew that there was a football stadium close to the allotment, but you had never heard any noise from there before. It must be a match day. Fulham versus… You didn't know who. Playing at Craven Cottage, their stadium alongside the Thames. It sounded like kick-off. Saturday, three o'clock. You listen to the ebb and flow of noise, trying to interpret the action on the pitch by the corresponding response of the crowd. Standing still, you begin to feel cold. You slip your arms through the short sleeves of the green gilet and allow the padded quilting to encase your back like the knobbly carapace of a garden bug. There is another loud cheer from the crowd. You take it as an affirmation of your actions.

Chapter Eight

Beneath the Hatch

It's something you've been putting off for far too long. In part, your inaction has been a pragmatic response to remaining secure; but, as the events of the previous day have come to teach you, perversely, your inaction is now threatening that same security, which you have sought to preserve.

The hatch in the floor of the shed is about two feet long by about a foot and a half wide. It is metallic, set in a surround of vulcanised rubber, where the rest of the floor is comprised of regular wooden boards. Close to each end of the hatch are matching depressions in the metal, not dissimilar to keyholes, but which are merely meant to be used as anchorage points for a handle to be inserted. You have already tried to subvert the need of this handle by attempting to prize your fingertips into the tiny crevice between the metal and the rubber seal, but the gap is too narrow and the metal lid too heavy, and you have not been able to gain any kind of purchase. You momentarily break off from your activity and go back into the lounge, to look out of the window.

This is your dilemma. Time spent away from your observation post at the window risks someone approaching the summerhouse unnoticed and surprising you; whilst time spent staring out of the window means that you are unable to explore the full limits of your surroundings. In the past, there had been no such dilemma. When you had been on guard duty it had been under orders from a higher command; it would have been under pain of death for you ever to have abandoned your post. Perhaps that is what is confusing your decision now? Some misplaced adherence to actions learned from loyalty to a past regime? It is hard to break the habits instilled over a lifetime.

There is no one to instruct you now. You have a form of freedom, although it may not be the one you once dreamed about. Part of that freedom is having to make decisions for yourself. Weighing up the relative risks associated with one action over another. Once again, you need to work with your engineer's problem-solving mind. Ever since you first discovered the summerhouse—how long is it now? One week; ten days? More?––you have only once had a visitor who has had the potential to threaten your occupancy. One visitor in ten days. If the past can be considered a blueprint for the future, it would suggest that you are unlikely to be disturbed by another visitor until a similar duration of time has passed. You are aware that this is not a particularly logical progression of thought. You are working on the gambler's fallacy: the erroneous belief that just because an event has happened in the past it is less likely to happen again in the immediate future. It is the same fallacy that makes casinos rich. The fact is that the older man might return again at any moment; or the tall man might enquire after his missing green gilet; or someone entirely new could pop up unannounced and unexpected. However, you do not want to live under this constant sense of anticipatory anxiety. You had had enough of that in the past. There are sufficient genuine worries without constructing potential imaginary ones. In your back pocket, you reach for a coin. You toss it up into the air, catching it neatly in your palm before transferring it to the back of your other hand. Heads or tails? Heads you continue exploring in the shed; tails you continue watching from the window. Tails. Best of three. Perhaps it will be heads next time. Tails. One more try. It must surely be heads next time; three tails on the trot would be most unlikely. Tails. The choice is made. You give one last swift glance outside the window and return to your work in the shed. If nothing else, it has taught you that it is never a good idea to trust any important decision to luck.

The tool for opening the hatch cover was in the same toolbox where yesterday you had discovered the screwdriver. There were two of them, identical in size and shape, both lurking near the bottom of the box, as though they had not been used lately. They were made of black-painted iron, and resembled a narrow anchor in shape, with a T-handle at one end and a rounded D-shape at the other. It was possible to fit this D-shape into the depression in the hatch cover and, by rotating it ninety degrees secure it in place so that it formed a handle. It would have been an easier job with two men but, by fixing a handle at either end of the hatch and positioning yourself central to them, you were able to lift the hatch directly up, and then swing it around in an arc so you could rest it on the floor next to its original position.

On first inspection, the opening revealed was rather disappointing. You don't know quite what you were expecting. In your imagination, you know that you had begun to build up a fantasy surrounding the hatch whereby it would at least link up with a short service tunnel that exited beyond the boundaries of the summerhouse; at most, that it would be the secret gateway to an entire subterranean realm, linking to the London sewer network, the underground railway and the civil defence shelters. The possibility of bursting these mental constructions had contributed much to your delay in exploring earlier. You know all too painfully the importance of hope, and the anguish when all hope is lost.

Of course, the reality is what you had always suspected. The hatch concealed a small pit, which gave access to some of the utilities that led into the summerhouse. There were the wires for the electrics, the pipes for the plumbing, and a stopcock to be able to turn on and off the water supply. The stopcock itself was housed in a sealed channel, attached to a supply and communication pipe at the bottom, which kept it protected from the outside but, unusually, there was quite a large area of bare earth surrounding this construction; an area that appeared as though it could be enlarged without too much difficulty.

A gardener's hand trowel, which was hanging on a peg on the wall of the shed, seemed like the ideal instrument. You began your excavation tentatively; nevertheless, it was only the matter of a few minutes' work before you had increased the size of the hole quite considerably, and had a conspicuous mound of loose earth piled up on the floorboards beside you. That wouldn't do. If you wanted to carry on working, you were going to have to plan ahead. There was an old iron bucket on the floor, beside the toolbox. You shovelled up the loose earth into this bucket, almost filling it to the brim; brushing the remaining bits of soil back down the hole so that they were not conspicuous. You then replaced the hatch cover, pleased to see that there was no superficial sign of your excavations. In your mind, the hatch and the hole offered distinct possibilities. Now that you had recalibrated your imagination, you could begin to work on the reality of the situation, rather than be distracted by the fantasy. You were going to need a few more tools for starters, some wood… it would be good to make a list but before you could do that, you were also going to need a pen and some paper.

There is one thing that you can do without waiting: you need to locate a good place where you can deposit freshly turned earth without it being conspicuous, first a bucketful but, after that, perhaps a whole lot more. The first bucket would be easy enough to distribute across the site where you had buried the dead man but, if you carried on with your digging, it would not be long before you had created a noticeable mound. Another solution is required. You rub your hands together in happy anticipation. It is a long time since you have been faced with a challenge entirely of your own making; a chance to shape and control your environment. You experience the memory of a feeling, which has long laid dormant within you, and which, at first, you almost struggle to identify: it is the feeling of autonomy.

Chapter Nine

Changing Identities

The white cat has been shitting underneath your cloches. The discovery of the foul-smelling deposit is unaccountably depressing. You wonder if there is anything that you can put down that might detract it. You are sure that some of the other allotment owners would know, but you are not in a position where you can ask any of them for advice. However, you are not going to let the minor irritation distract you from the agenda of the day. You have a lot to do, and the nervous apprehension of someone who is not sure that they have the abilities to carry out all the necessary tasks.

You had spent the previous evening planning the next day's schedule. Although your explorations beneath the hatch had crystallised your ideas, for several days now you had been of the opinion that, if you were going to make the summerhouse anything more than just another passing abode; somewhere grander than just a temporary shelter where you lay your head, you were going to have to venture out into the world beyond the allotment again. There were things that needed buying and, with the cash from Alfred Wurgihurt's wallet, you had the means to make this possible.

You had already checked off on a mental checklist all the items that you were going to need from the summerhouse that day, but there was no harm in running through them one more time, just to be sure. A good engineer knows that you can never have too much preparation.

The seven ten-pound notes were in your back pocket. Check. Along with the small quantity of loose change. In a plastic bag, which you had discovered in the shed, you had placed the brown brogue shoes and the tall man's green gilet jacket. Check. You had toyed with bringing the dead man's bank card with you but, in the end, decided against the idea. Some last residue of guilt still attached itself to the possession of the card, and it formed an all too obvious link to the dead man, which you were not yet in any position to explain.

Leaving the allotment afforded you a sudden moment of panic; it felt as though you were severing a link with a place of safety, even though you knew, rationally, that if your plan went well, you would be returning again in only a matter of a few hours. Seeing the busy streets beyond the main gate of the allotments brought on a sensation akin to agoraphobia, and it was only with a conscious mental effort that you forced yourself to continue. You steadied yourself against the high brick wall, which surrounds the allotments, and took a deep breath before continuing.

The noise of the city closed in on you like an approaching tube train. You had almost forgotten the conflict of sounds that had once been the soundtrack to your daily life: the car engines; horns beeping; distant sirens; people talking. In the allotments, you had become used to the quiet tranquillity of nature; all the raucous confusion of the streets was exiled to the extremities, boxed and contained, never more than a distant background accompaniment to a more peaceful, melodic tune.

The river is to your left, but you are not yet ready for it. First you need to make a few essential purchases. At the point where Bishop's Avenue meets Fulham Palace Road there is a small parade of local shops: a coffee shop; an estate agent; a beauty salon; a charity shop, and a small, cut-price supermarket. The supermarket would appear to hold out the best hope of what you are looking for. You cross the road, and approach the shop cautiously. You are conscious of your appearance; don't want to risk being ejected before you have had a chance to show the colour of your money. You enter the shop in the wake of two middle-aged women, who are chatting animatedly. No one appears to notice you. Living on the streets, you get used to being invisible. There is a stratum running through the city, each band as clearly demarcated one from the other as bands of sedimentary rock through a Jurassic cliff face. The homeless occupy a stratum close to the ground; a narrow, heavily-impacted strip, squeezed and pushed to the margins. Above it lies the wide strata of everyday life: the shoppers; the office workers; the tourists; the home-owners. There is no point where the two strata converge; forever destined to run on parallel lines, the one stepping on the other, oblivious, uncaring. And above it all? Another stratum. Out of sight; out of touch, like a fourth dimension. Whilst you remain in your own stratum, you are ignored. However, experience has taught you that the blanket of invisibility, which seems to cloak you for as long as you remain in your allotted space in the gutter, is very soon stripped from your shoulders as soon as you dare to venture beyond the parameters of expectation. You move from being the pupil in the back row of the classroom with their eyes averted, hoping not to meet the teacher's gaze, to the eager student sitting in the middle of the front row with their hand stuck firmly up, desperate to be chosen to answer the next question: "Me, sir; me, sir."

"Yes, sir, what can I do for you?"

There is a suspicion of condescension in the shop assistant's voice, but you have already spotted the aisle of goods you seek, and you manage to wave his unwelcome attention's away with a vague shake of your hand. There is not a great deal of choice, but you are purely seeking utility not fine design. Once you have made your selection, you wave your purchases in the direction of the same shop assistant, who continues to watch you, clearly determined to watch the goods all the way from shelf to cash register.

The cashier displays no similar conscientiousness. She yawns, loud and open-mouthed, mindlessly passing your items across a bar scanner. She doesn't even bother to tell you the total to pay; simply swivels a display in your direction so that you can read the price: £3.92. You hand over one of your ten-pound notes.

"Plastic bag?"

You look blank.

"Do you want a plastic bag? It's five pence extra."

You wave your hand again; it is the same vague 'keep away' gesture that you had used on the shop assistant. This time it receives a dismissive shrug of the shoulders, and the cashier moves on to her next customer. You take your change, and scoop up your purchases, tumbling them into your own bag on top of the tall man's green gilet: a safety razor, a bar of soap, deodorant, and a small hand mirror. It is a small start on the road to a large transformation.

Back outside, in the street, a display in the window of the charity shop makes you pause. A battered-looking mannequin, with moulded hair and wearing a startled expression beneath its carved eyebrows, is putting up a good fight against being dressed by an elderly woman volunteer. With arms obstinately inflexible and a torso stubbornly rigid, the shop dummy is resisting all attempts to be kitted out in a hideous ensemble of clashing garments. The elderly woman is red in the face from her exertions; she waves at you angrily through the glass when she spots that she has gained an audience. However, it is not the comic tableaux, but several displays of second hand clothes hanging on wheeled rails beyond that have made you stand and stare. The shop door opens to the accompaniment of an old-fashioned bell, and you are instantly struck by the powerful smell of ammonia, like that of an industrial laundry. In a backroom, you can see someone working at a steam cleaner, stooping to pick up clothes, which have spilt from a large bag to spread out all over the floor. The rails of clothes have been divided up into those for men and those for women. The women's racks are characterised by a mad medley of shocking assorted colours, flimsy material and sheer fabrics; in complete contrast, the men's garments appear uniformly brown, thick, coarse cloth and generously oversized. It takes you several minutes of perusing, but you eventually pick out two shirts and a pair of trousers, which look as though they were designed for a human being and not for a mountain silverback gorilla. From another rail, you select a couple of pairs of white underpants—you would have preferred boxer shorts, but there is no choice in your size—and a couple of pairs of dark socks, with a Paisley print pattern. On a sudden whim, you also add a tie to your selection. It has black and blue diagonal stripes, which reminds you of a football shirt you had when you were a child. The elderly woman steps out of the window display to serve you; she is still looking bad-tempered. Her hair is melded into an unflattering silver helmet, not dissimilar to that of the mannequin. The items are rung up on the till and, wordlessly, you hand over two ten-pound notes.

"Have you got anything smaller?"

You look blank.

The elderly woman waves one of the notes at you:

"Any change? Oh, never mind."

With over-elaborate pantomime, she counts out your change.

"A bag?"

You nod, reaching into your back pocket for a five-pence piece.

"Free of charge, luvvie."

The elderly woman laughs uproariously as though she has cracked a huge joke. You can still hear her voice as you leave the shop; the clang off the bell sounding behind you: "Free of charge, luvvie."

You retrace your steps, recross the road, and head back past the main gate of the allotments, barely halting in your stride to glance inside. Your next appointment is at the opposite end of the street. Automatically, you glance to your wrist and a watch that does not exist. You have no way of knowing if you are keeping to the schedule that you have set for yourself, but you feel as though you have not wasted time.

The Bishops Park public toilets occupy a small building, which resembles a detached brick bungalow, with a steep-sided triangular roof and a green front door. Inside, the gents' toilet contains two cream-painted cubicles, a white porcelain sink and a long urinal, draining into a single sluice on the floor, sub-divided by bulky porcelain slabs, which superficially make the entire structure resemble an old fashioned, steel-column radiator. It is surprisingly clean; well maintained; a testament to the council tax paid by the residents of one of London's wealthiest boroughs. You make a mental note to make more use of the facilities; they are a step up from where you have been currently taking a shit.

You are aware that you have revealed where it is that you go when you want to piss—the tall shrubs, which grow directly outside the summerhouse door—but you have said nothing about where you take a shit. Some things seem too personal to discuss; too private; not something that you care to share with a wider audience. Your time living on the streets has brought upon you your fair share of unavoidable humiliations and degradations, you don't choose to voluntarily debase yourself any further than is absolutely necessary by revealing the intimacies of all your toilet habits. There are some things, which are simply best kept secret, like Barry Robins' gimmick.

You cast a second appraising glance upon the sterile cubicles, but instantly dismiss them from your mind. You do not want to get sidetracked from your main task and, the simple fact is, that you do not need to go and, experience has taught you that, when you do not need to go nothing on earth is going to alter that position.

You stand by the wash basin; place your two bags on the tiled floor at your feet. It is quite dry; recently cleaned. These toilets are regularly inspected. There is a wipe-clean duty rota, contained within a hard plastic sheath hanging on the back of the toilet door, which would confirm the fact, but you do not bother to read it. There is no mirror above the wash basin, but you have anticipated this likelihood. It is your engineer's training again: planning ahead. You rummage in the top of the first bag, removing the purchases that you made in the supermarket. You lay the soap and hand mirror on the back of the basin, and remove one of the disposable razors from its plastic wrapping. You run a hand across your chin, tugging the long hairs downwards, brushing and straightening them. You have always found it easy to grow a beard. You had first shaved when you were only eleven years old. As an adult, you would often shave twice a day to maintain a clean-shaven appearance. Left unchecked, your beard tended to grow in slightly uneven clumps, and this was the face that now stared back at you from the small hand mirror. You looked thinner than you remembered. Your eyes more sunken; suspicious pools peering out from beneath hooded lids. Your skin looked sallow, too; pale and loose, as though it belonged to someone different; someone older.

You attack the beard with the razor, instantly wishing that you had had the foresight to purchase a pair of scissors to trim the longest hairs first: engineer's training at fault for once. However, by pulling the hair taut, you are able to run the razor across the longest strands and gradually reduce the overall mass of growth. The white porcelain bowl of the small sink quickly disappears beneath a shower of long black bristles. The basin looks like some kind of physics experiment involving iron filings; the little black quills all lining up like a regiment, ready to be swished away down the plughole. With the longest hairs despatched, you begin to run the razor across your skin, swathing through the dark stubble, turning your pallid skin red with the friction of the sharp blade across your chin, cheeks and top lip. You lather up a handful of soap and spread the frothy bubbles across your face, feeling an instant cooling to the sensation of burning. You turn on both taps, whishing your hands around the bowl, creating a vortex to suck in all the loose hairs. You splash your face; reappraising the new reflection in the mirror. If anything, you look even more emaciated than before. There is still the ghost of a beard remaining, but you have learned from experience that no amount of shaving will ever remove that; like your shadow, it is an eternal companion that you have come to live with. You run your hand back over your chin.

It still feels rather stubbly, but it is a definite improvement. You look different to before. Not necessarily better, but different, and that had been the effect that you had been hoping to achieve. Carefully, you pack away the toiletries, repacking the soap into its original plastic packaging, so that it does not make a slimy mess in the bag, and examine the purchases you had made at the charity shop: stage two of your transformation.

You have the toilets entirely to yourself, nevertheless you decide that the extra privacy of one of the cubicles is necessary for the exchange of your clothing. You choose the one on the far left, closest to the outside wall and furthest from the urinals. Inside, the space is limited for any major physical manoeuvres, but you are pleased to see that the cubicle has a functioning latch; there is even a near-full roll of toilet paper, which you make a private note to steal before leaving. Alongside your previous crimes, you do not consider that this minor misdemeanour will greatly affect your positioning on the grand graph of criminality. There is a small plastic hook on the back of the toilet door, and you hang your two new shirts, the pair of trousers, and the green gilet upon it, adding the black and blue striped tie over the top. You are particularly pleased with the tie. It is a touch of class. A superfluous frippery, which speaks conformity louder than any ostentatious display of bank notes. On the floor of the cubicle, you place the pair of brown brogues, balancing on top of them your new socks and underpants. It feels almost like a surfeit of clothing, each item neatly folded, pressed and ironed. Swiftly, you strip off all your own clothes, packing them into one of the now empty bags, until you stand naked in the small cubicle. You take your time dressing, enjoying the luxury of new garments. The trousers are a little loose at the waist, but nothing that a belt or a decent meal couldn't fix. You have almost forgotten how to tie a tie; it is so long since you last wore one. Your first attempt leaves you helplessly flapping left over right and right over left without knowing what to do with either end, and your second effort produces a knot in the right place, but with the front section of the tie hopelessly shorter than the rear one. You had always imagined that this was one of those things that once learned you never forgot. Like riding a bicycle. Or sex. The third attempt is better. You look down to admire your new self. You are a different man to the one who left the summerhouse that morning. The final item of clothing that you put on is the green padded gilet. It wouldn't have been your own choice of garments, but as the completion of a disguise it has its benefits

Exiting the cubicle, and had you ever been brought up watching the TV show as a child, you might have been put in mind of Mr Benn but, like Robin Hood, the Great Train Robbery, and Peter Rabbit, it was simply another cultural reference, which was outside of your ken. Mr Benn Goes Cottaging.

Before you leave the toilets altogether, you take one last look at your face in the small hand mirror. You are pleased by what you see. Smiling back at you is the new, clean-shaven face of Alfred Wurgihurt.

Chapter Ten

The Bridge

You are still conscious of your security. Or, more to the point, your lack of it. Doing any work in the shed, or at the hatch, still requires you to leave the entrance to the summerhouse unattended, so that anyone could walk in. A new lock on the front door is required, but the door itself is of too flimsy a construction to take either a mortice or a lever-style lock. It might look too ostentatious, too, as though you have got something to hide. A simple chain would do the trick; just something that you can fasten from inside the summerhouse, which would prevent any surprise visits from unwelcome intruders. It means another trip beyond the allotments. To the 'outside world', as you have come to think of it. In truth, you have been looking for just such an excuse to make another trip. Around the summerhouse, you tend to stick to wearing your old clothes, existing within your own skin and your own thoughts, whereas an excursion beyond the allotment walls is an opportunity to adopt your Alfred Wurgihurt persona; to make use of your new outfit, and to exist within someone else's head for a brief period of time.

There are other things you could do with buying, too. Some progress has been made digging down beneath the hatch, but it is slow going. A powerful torch would be beneficial as, too, would a decent chisel. In the direction you have been digging, you have encountered a barrier of bricks, and a chisel would be useful in order to break through them. You have searched Alfred Wurgihurt's toolbox, but it doesn't contain anything suitable: you guess, it is not something that would have been needed for the day-to-day maintenance of the allotment. You don't know how far the barrier of bricks extend, but they are proving an immoveable obstruction given the current tools available to you and, if you are not able to remove them, it would mean abandoning your current dig and going back to square one and starting off in a new direction. When you had worked as an engineer, you would have had detailed plans to foresee these kind of difficulties; would have had professional equipment in order to surmount them. Now, you were back to basics, equipped with nothing more than a lifetime of acquired knowledge and a few rudimentary tools. There was something quite honourable in this return to fundamental principles but, at the same time, you have no intention of becoming a martyr to industry when a bit of simple kit could save you both a lot of time and a lot of elbow-grease.

You have talked yourself into it, not that you needed any convincing. Another trip to the shops is required. You still have the greater portion of Alfred Wurgihurt's seventy pounds remaining. Be prudent with your purchases, and you might even have a bit of cash left over to buy a proper meal. The produce of the allotments was proving adequate staple fare, but you were conscious that it had been some considerable time since you had eaten anything in the way of protein. Once or twice when you had been working at the hatch you had suddenly felt slightly lightheaded; once you had had to stop work entirely, sit up and rest because you had suddenly felt nauseous, and that sign of weakness could be down to an imbalance of nutrients in your diet. One night, you had dreamed about eating a steak. A plump, rare, succulent steak, where the blood ran freely from it at the first cut of the knife, leaving a reddening pool to slow seep across the white porcelain of your plate, in the same way that the blood of your neighbours had left their indelible mark on the pavements of your bombed homeland. Regardless of how your dreams began, this was the way your dreams always ended.

You felt that you were sufficiently well acquainted with the shops at the north end of Bishop's Park Road to know that they did not stock the kind of items you were seeking. It was time for Alfred Wurgihurt to strike out to pastures new. It was time for him to cross the bridge.

You began to don your disguise. Brown brogues, white shirt, new trousers, striped tie, green gilet. Except was it a disguise, or was this simply a different manifestation of an old you; one that had not had the chance to see the light of day in this new country? When you had worked as an engineer, you had always dressed smartly; more smartly than the charity shop hand-me-downs that you treat with such reverence today. You used to wear suits that had been specially tailored for you; good fabrics; internationally renowned brands. Alfred Wurgihurt is a poor relation to your previous self, but he is all that you have; a stepping stone to a better life. A former life.

You sweep up the remaining notes and change from the top of the sideboard; consider taking the entire wallet; decide against it; consider taking Alfred Wurgihurt's credit card; decide that you might as well; slip it into the back pocket of your trousers.

There is someone walking along the path directly outside your allotment. You have become too casual taking precautions before exiting; this time, you hadn't even so much as glanced outside the window before you opened the door of the summerhouse. You have allowed your Alfred Wurgihurt persona too great an ascendancy; begun to believe that you are not an imposter. It is a dangerous precedence. There is nothing you can do now. The other person has spotted you. You must just bluff it out; pretend that there is nothing wrong. You nod companionably at one another; two fellow allotment owners passing the time of day. Nothing to be seen here. The danger is over. The other person displayed not the least suspicion about you; London indifference overriding neighbourly interest. It is a warning to you, though. You cannot afford to lessen your guard for a moment. It is a moment of realisation, too. Your concern stems from the fact that you now have something to lose. It would be foolish to throw away everything that you have built up in the last few weeks for a moment's lapse of concentration.

Chastened, you fasten the padlock to the summerhouse door, glancing left and right before you make your way to the main gates of the allotments. You turn left onto the road, past the public toilets, and through an old stone gateway, which would once have been part of the original Fulham Palace, onto a public footpath, before turning left again onto a pleasant path, which runs through a narrow strip of parkland immediately adjacent to the river. The river is wide here and, today, the water level is high and the currents fast moving. On the opposite bank, you can see the long concrete slipway into the water, from where the rowing clubs launch their boats, and the lines of narrow, white-hulled vessels stowed upside-down on metal trailers, awaiting crews to transport them to the water. Further along, there is a tall, four-storey pub, and a short covered pier, dog-legging down to a big Dutch barge. It is typical of you to be looking to the distance when there are similar attractions on your own side of the river; your wife used to endlessly complain of you that you were forever seeking for where the grass is greener, rather than appreciating what it is that you have under your nose; it is a lesson that you do not fully learn until you have experienced loss.

The bridge is a five-span structure of white stone. It appears unnaturally low in the water, as though there is not enough room for any vessel to pass beneath one of its arches, but this illusion is caused simply by virtue of its considerable length, the one distance foreshortening the other. You watch as a line of five tall, red double-decker buses cross the bridge, one after another, small faces gazing out across the river from each window, the wheels of the buses invisible beneath the bridge's parapet.

Your footpath leads you to the foot of one of the solid stone towers that supports the bridge before veering left and around, and onto the bridge itself. You pause briefly, leaning on a four-bar metal railing, staring into the black depths of the water. The green paint of the top railing has been worn shiny and smooth by the thousands of people who have stopped in the self-same spot to do exactly the same thing before you. Under the bridge, little eddies have formed in the water; mini whirlpools disrupting the river's even flow. Directly beneath you, close to the water, is a rounded concrete platform, which provides the base to the first stone span. It is a little island in the water, strangely inviting, cut off from the main thoroughfare of people. It wouldn't be difficult to scale the railings and drop down onto the little concrete island; experience that same sense of proprietorship that you feel in the summerhouse of a territory that you have colonised and conquered for yourself, but you are aware that it would only draw unwelcome attention to yourself, when discretion is still your best disguise. There will be other opportunities and alternative Arcadias for you to conquer in the future, but now is not the time for expanding your empire. Immediately beside you, there is an official inscription carved into the surface of one of the stone slabs. It is weathered with age and quite difficult to read, but you trace out each letter with your finger, feeling the chiselled, indented characters like a blind person reading braille: Sir J. W. Bazalgette G.B. Edward Bazalgette Esq., Engineers, 1886. 1886 or 1888? You are not sure. Someone has chipped away at the date, leaving it slightly obscured. You have never heard of Bazalgette. Neither Sir J. W. or Edward Esq. Nevertheless, you find yourself feeling a certain kinship with them. Engineers. One and all.

Digression Ten.One
Putney Bridge

Similar to Fulham Palace, Putney Bridge is blessed with its own tourist information panel, which provides the interested and the unacquainted with a potted snapshot of its construction, history, curiosities and importance. You are becoming something of a doyen of these information boards; the boards themselves often holding a greater fascination for you than the thing they are actually describing.

The current stone bridge was constructed in 1886—1886 then, not 1888—and replaced an earlier wooden one completed in 1729. The engineer behind the new construction is credited as Joseph Bazalgette—Sir J. W., you presume. You wonder where Edward Esq. fits into the picture? The bridge is notable for being the starting point for the annual boat race between the teams of Cambridge and Oxford universities; the place where women's rights advocate Mary Wollstonecraft threatened to commit suicide—you are not sure if that is notable, or not?—and where serial killer John Christie was apprehended and arrested—you find that more notable; your tastes have always veered more towards the tabloid than the broadsheet.

Either end of the bridge is abutted by a medieval parish church: St Mary's, Putney to the south and All

Saints, Fulham to the north. You must have passed it without noticing. More interesting to you, is the fact that there are two locked cages beneath the bridge. Popular legend states that these cages where used for drowning criminals. Your tabloid sensibility rather liked the sound of that. However, the broadsheet reality is more mundane: the cages simply prevented access to two storm relief outlets to the London sewer system; another engineering initiative of the industrious Sir Joseph Bazalgette. You find yourself somehow liking him less.

• • •

Looking out from the centre of the bridge feels like standing at the bow of a big ship. Strangely, though, you feel less connected with the river than you had done looking down on your concrete island, and more united with the road. The calm quiet of the water is replaced by the overriding noise of traffic, and the boats that pass beneath your arch seem part of a different world, immeasurably separated from you. You are conscious of a point of transition: not just the river and the road, but also the two sides of the land itself; north and south. You have crossed from the north bank of the Thames; stand at an interim point before passing over to the south bank of the Thames. It is a point of transition for Alfred Wurgihurt, too. On the north bank, he has always had to walk in the shadows, scared that he might be recognised; on the south bank, he is known by no one. Take one step to your left, and Alfred Wurgihurt is a free man.

Chapter Eleven

A Slap-up Meal

You are still conscious of your list of chores. Even a free man finds himself with jobs to do. A chain for the front door, a powerful torch, and a chisel. You are not quite sure where is the best place to find any of these items. You have discovered plenty of shops on the south side of the river, but none of them look like the kind of place that would stock what you are looking for. There are shops selling frou-frous and shops selling knick-knacks; shops stocking bric-a-brac and others specialising in gewgaws; windows of trinkets and baubles and novelties and thingamajigs, but very few selling anything vaguely useful. Until, that is, you discovered Putney Hardware, a neutron star of practicality; densely packed from floor to ceiling with tools and tackle and screws and sockets, as though the premises themselves exerted a strong magnetic pull, which had drawn in every loose metallic object from the surrounding streets. Here you were spoilt for choice in your selection of a door chain—"Brass or metallic, sir? Standard or lockable?"—and with your torch—"Battery or rechargeable, sir? LED or Laser?"—and even your chisel—"Flat of cross-cut, sir? Round nose or diamond point?". In the end, you left with a standard metallic door chain, a pocket-sized Maglite, a large stone chisel, suitable for cutting bricks, and the promise that you would return whenever you planned to make any further improvements to the summerhouse.

Emerging from the dark and claustrophobic interior of the shop into the bright daylight, you suddenly experience another bout of lightheadedness, which has you stumbling in your stride. You bend over double, breathing in large gasps of traffic-soaked air, waiting for the lights in your eyes to cease flashing, uncaring of the appalled and suspicious stares of passers-by. One young woman stops, places a tentative hand on your back, and asks if you are okay, but you silently wave her away, trying to indicate that you are fine. She does not pursue the enquiry. The moment of dizziness soon passes, but it is another wake-up call. You neglect your health at your peril. Even though you have always prided yourself on being fit both in body and in mind, it only takes a brief period of living rough to reduce both your physical and your mental wellbeing to tatters.

Across the road, there are chairs on the pavement; tables laid for dinner; tablecloths and menus. You cannot remember the last time that you ate out at a restaurant. It would have been to celebrate a special occasion; back in your homeland; all the family present. It was a different life. A different person. To eat in a restaurant purely for the sake of satisfying your appetite seems like an extravagance beyond contemplation. Except, perhaps there is cause for celebration? It is not every day that you acquire a new chain for your door, a torch and a chisel. You need little persuasion.

A young waitress has the door to the restaurant open for you before you are even halfway across the road. You accept the offer of a table inside; less conspicuous than sitting outside on the pavement, subject to the vagaries of the British weather and the unvoiced judgements of every passing stranger.

The menu arrives in a large padded binding, which disguises the rather limited selection written in an italic script and contained on a single sheet of A4. The wine menu is separate, and is more extensive. Automatically, you wave the wine menu away, before having second thoughts. In for a penny. You run your finger down the choice of dishes printed on the A4 sheet. Many of the words are not familiar to you, and you are wary of openly displaying your unfamiliarity with the language, conscious that Alfred Wurgihurt would not be similarly disadvantaged. The longer that you look at the list, the more the words simply blur and run together, forming one big unintelligible jumble, such that you cannot distinguish starters from main dishes, and desserts from drinks. You can feel a sensation of clamminess sweep over you again, similar to the lightheadedness you had experienced outside on the pavement, but now the cause is from fear, not from lack of food. You consider standing up and leaving, but you are conscious of making a scene. It feels as though the eyes of the entire restaurant are focused upon you; your every movement the object of intense scrutiny; your minutest gesture being analysed and commented upon. The waitress is watching you from behind her counter, keen to assist as soon as you have made a selection. You glance in her direction and she instinctively takes a step forward; you avert your gaze and she retreats again, as though there is a mechanical link, which joins the two distinct activities. You return your attention to the menu, now no more than a sheet of random words, surprised to suddenly see one phrase stand out clearly amidst the confusion and take conscious form inside your mind in the shape of something that you recognise as both tangible and, more importantly, edible. Steak *au poivre.* It is the French that you understand. Your father had spoken the language fluently, and he had taught you a basic vocabulary when you had been very little, knowing even then that it was a dying language in your homeland. Your finger hovers uncertainly over the words, like a mayfly over a springtime pond, and you look across to the waitress, anxious to attract her attention before the fleeting chimera of comprehension disappears again.

"And anything to start?"

There is a look of startled perplexity in your eyes, which the waitress is swift to exploit. She points to some words close to the top of the menu, and you find yourself nodding blankly.

"And a dessert?"

This time the waitress suggests something close to the bottom of the menu and, once again, you nod in amiable agreement, not knowing precisely what you are committing yourself to.

"Something to drink?"

The food menu is stowed away, and the wine menu produced in its place.

"Red or white?"

Pages flick back and forth, until the waitress's finger halts above a line of text. Instinctively, you scan across to the right-hand side of the page, attempting to read the price, but the waitress is too quick for you, and you have accepted her suggestion before thinking. You start to raise your hand to call her back, say that you have changed your mind but, once again, you do not want to draw unwanted attention to yourself and so you hold your tongue. It doesn't matter. After all, you had wanted a slap-up meal, and you were supposed to be celebrating. It is not every day that Alfred Wurgihurt ventures south of the river.

When it arrives, the wine is red, which pleases you, and an entire bottle, which does not. However, you meekly take a sip from the glass, which the waitress pours for you, and smile and nod to indicate that she should pour you some more. In fact, the wine is good. Very good. You had started to worry again about how much it will all cost when your starter arrives. It is a salad of avocado, beetroot and feta, which you would not have chosen for yourself if you had understood the menu better. The avocado is okay, but the beetroot has stained the cubes of feta pink, making them look like some kind of absorbent sponge, which has been used to mop up blood.

"Everything okay?"

You nod and smile again, raising your glass and showing your teeth.

Despite your reservations about the dish, you clear your plate; several times having to consciously slow yourself from appearing to wolf down the food too quickly. Your manners have suffered during your enforced time living on the streets; grubbing for food in bins at the back of restaurants after closing time, there was not a great deal of time for etiquette and social niceties; it was more a question of the survival of the fittest. You pour yourself another glass of wine from the bottle, which has been left on the table. You hold it up to the light, admiring the dark, ruby colour. What was it you had been told about wine in restaurants? If there were bubbles in it then it had been watered down? You can't see any bubbles, but you are no connoisseur. You down half the glass in one greedy mouthful. You could easily drink the rest in the same fashion but, once again, you moderate yourself; attempting to appear nonchalant, as if this is an event of little consequence for you.

Your good intentions swiftly vanish upon the arrival of the main course. The steak is red and rare, the way you like it; the meat tender and succulent, and the sauce well-cooked and tasty, and you fall upon the dish like a ravenous animal, as though you have not eaten for weeks. You can feel trickles of the brown, pepper sauce running down from your mouth and over your chin; find your head bowed lower to your plate; barely chewing the meat before swallowing and returning to cut off another mouthful. You are conscious that you must be presenting a disgracefully debauched spectacle of naked gluttony, but you don't care. For once in your life, you just don't care.

Digression Eleven.One

An Elizabethan Banquet

The year was 1601 when Queen Elizabeth I dined at Fulham Palace, and some of the manners displayed at the table would have made your own vulgar exhibition seem positively decorous in comparison.

Guests of honour at the feast were a delegation recently arrived from Denmark. It had been a period of strained relations, both diplomatically and economically, between England and the Danes, having culminated in Bishop Richard Bancroft travelling to Emden the previous year in a failed attempt to settle the dispute, which existed between the two countries.

Certainly, there was no shortage of food or hospitality. The menu made your own choice of steak *au poivre* appear very modest. The first course was a pottage of oats, vegetables and beans, which was thick enough to stand a spoon up in. Following this was jugged hare, in a sauce thickened by the animal's own blood, a quarter of venison and a loin of veal, swiftly followed by two pies, each stuffed with a variety of game-birds, and seasoned by saffron and cloves. The fish course consisted of a huge sturgeon cooked in parsley and vinegar, and accompanied by a shoal of pike, served with oysters and liquor. A whole wild boar, spit-roasted, provided the main course, and then for dessert there was a red and white chequerboard of leach—a milk-based jelly of rosewater and sugar—and various sweetmeats, Norfolk fool and crystallised fruits, all washed down by copious wine and ales.

The Danes were suitably impressed. Where ecclesiastical negotiations had failed the year before, it looked as though a good old-fashioned Tudor bender might be all that was required in order to restore diplomatic relations.

• • •

Your own dessert course had arrived. It was a raspberry tiramisu. If you were being particularly fussy, you would have either preferred the raspberries on their own or the tiramisu on its own; for you, combining the two elements has the effect of diminishing both of them, but it is a long time since you have eaten anything quite so sweet, and just as a pure sugar rush you give the dessert a thumbs-up. There is still quite a lot of wine left in the bottle. You are in no rush. You pour yourself another large glass, and sit back from the table, overly replete.

"Coffee?"

Why not? Alfred Wurgihurt is a man of leisure. A man who can sit and sip his coffee; a man who can take his time to enjoy the reminder of his bottle of wine; a man who… has spent most of his remaining cash on a standard metallic door chain, a pocket-sized Maglite, and a large stone chisel, suitable for cutting bricks.

Chapter Twelve

Should You Stay, or Should You Go?

Your coffee arrived, cooled, was drunk, and the cup taken away again. There is still a tiny dribble of wine left in the bottom of the bottle, but it must be obvious to anyone that you are drinking it more slowly now, deliberately spinning out the time before the fateful moment when the bill for the meal will be presented to you; already, the waitress has twice attempted to remove the bottle from your table assuming it to be empty, and twice you have managed to check her.

You find yourself sizing up the distance between your chair and the door, and trying to work out how long it would take you to cross the restaurant floor, if you decide to make a dash for it. There were several potential hazards to overcome; a couple of spare chairs in your way; your uncertainty as to whether the door opens inwards or outwards. On such little details rests the difference between escape and apprehension. Then, even if you made it outside, would anyone give chase? And for how long? The young waitress did not look like someone who would care unduly if you scarpered without paying, but you had been conscious of the recent appearance of a couple of 'heavies' from the kitchen, who were lurking behind the counter for no discernible reason, and whom kept casting suspicious glances in your direction. Perhaps they can sense that you have a bit of form when it comes to leaving without paying; at times, living on the streets, it had been a daily necessity; part of your arsenal for survival. There had been those cups of coffee and muffins from Starbucks; a quiche from Pret; even several pasties from Greggs. On your scale of thieving, you knew that none of these crimes represented your finest hour, but you felt as though you could have justified each one should you have been required in a court of law. In each case, you had been hungry; relatively modest in your acquisitions; only taking what you could eat in one sitting, much like an animal in the wild. The circumstances were slightly different now: the meal that you had just consumed must have cost a fortune—only now do you recognise the scale of your indulgence; you had carried on eating even beyond the point when you had felt full—the simple truth is that you feel positively bloated, so much so that you doubt your ability to make a clean getaway on such a full stomach; and no judge in the country would consider a raspberry tiramisu and an entire bottle of expensive Rioja a requisite purely to satisfy the nutritional requirements of a hungry man.

You upend the bottle over your glass, even banging the end in the forlorn hope that it will release a few extra drops, but you still only manage to extract a sparse quantity of liquid, barely sufficient to cover the bottom of your glass, and a couple of residue lumps of red sediment, which look like congealed blood as they stick to the side of your glass before slowly sliding down the side. The waitress is a keen witness to this unedifying spectacle, swooping in on the empty bottle with uncharacteristic decisiveness; leaving in its place an ominously folded piece of paper.

"Your bill, sir."

You cannot delay any longer. You must make a decision. Should you stay, or should you go? If you go, there will be trouble. And if you stay, it will be double. Should you cool it, or should you blow?

You half rise from your seat. The motion causes the 'heavies' behind the counter to turn in your direction as though in synchronicity. You sit back down, and the 'heavies' similarly subside. The waitress is being sent out as an advanced guard; she approaches you with something held in her hand. It looks rather like a Taser. You wonder if they are planning to not wait for you to incriminate yourself before they make a citizen's arrest. As she approaches closer, you realise that the Taser is a portable credit card machine.

"Pay by card, sir?"

Credit card? The possibility had not even occurred to you. It sparks a chain of thought, which has you instinctively reaching towards your back pocket. A credit card. Alfred Wurgihurt's credit card. Of course. It had been the last thing that you had taken with you when you had set out earlier that day from the summerhouse. You offer the thin lifeline of plastic.

The waitress takes the card, inserts it into the base of the machine, presses a button, and then hands the machine to you, discretely taking a step backwards and looking towards the floor:

"PIN, sir?"

PIN? What is the PIN? You remember discovering the small slip of paper where Alfred Wurgihurt had recorded it, but that had been several weeks ago now. You had refolded the slip and returned it to Alfred Wurgihurt's wallet, and you didn't have his wallet with you. You were going to have to rely on memory. Four numbers. They were the same four numbers that formed the combination of the lock to the summerhouse door; Alfred Wurgihurt had clearly not been someone who had relied on the security of having multiple passwords or codes. You have used the combination of the summerhouse door so many times now that it has become almost second nature to you; something automatic that you no longer consciously register. In other circumstances, the numbers would have been available to you instantly, but under the pressure-cooker atmosphere of the restaurant, you can feel your mind becoming blank, the four digits receding into hidden depths of your memory, the more so the harder that you struggle to recall them. One of the 'heavies' has moved around to the near side of the counter, closer to you. You no longer have the option of a hurried exit, even should you have wished to choose it. The waitress looks up from where she has been attempting to preserve your privacy, prompting again:

"Your PIN?"

You look into her eyes. Does she see your desperation? Can she perceive the rush of conflicting thoughts and emotions, which are coursing through your body? You feel like a hunted criminal, finally cornered, with nowhere left to go; trapped and surrounded; the same feeling of insecurity and isolation that you had felt sleeping rough on the streets. But you are not that same man; times have changed; that is a life, which you have left behind.

You are Alfred Wurgihurt. A man with a credit card. Alfred Wurgihurt who eats out in fancy restaurants. Alfred Wurgihurt. A man with a PIN.

You stab four numbers into the portable credit card machine with decisiveness and authority, before handing it back to the young waitress. She looks at the message on the screen, before handing the machine back to you:

"I am afraid that's not the correct number, sir."

You feign surprise. The other 'heavy' has taken another step forward. Behind your ostentatious over-acting, your surprise is quite genuine. You were sure that you had remembered the correct numbers. There was a '4' and a '2' and a '6' and a '7'. The combination definitely began with a '4' and definitely ended with a '7'. Had you muddled the middle two numbers? '2' before '6'? Or '6' before '2'? The more you repeat the two possibilities, the more they become confused in your mind. You stab in the four numbers into the machine again. This time, you don't even know yourself in which order you have pressed the keys; you have allowed your instincts to direct you; have relied on the pattern of movement of your fingers over the conscious recognition of the digits.

The waitress takes a step back from your table, her attention once again focussed on the screen of the machine. The two 'heavies' are flanking her, one on either side, like the bodyguard to a precious object.

You are conscious of a tinny, whirring sound. The small machine is spewing out a thin curl of paper. The waitress removes your credit card from the machine, tears off the roll of paper, and hands both items to you, smiling:

"Thank you, Mr Wright."

You almost correct her and tell her that it is pronounced 'Wurgihurt', but you decide to let it go. Instead, you feel around in your pocket for the loose change that you have left over from your purchases in the hardware store. It doesn't add up to very much, but you leave it on the table as a tip.

Chapter Thirteen

No Lessons to be Learned from Old War Movies

The bricks you have excavated beneath the hatch are something of a mystery. For one thing, they are a lot smaller than traditional house bricks; for another, what are they doing so far underground?

You are conscious that you have not sat back to reflect upon the progress of your excavations for a number of days. The fact is, the nature of your project has developed and evolved in direct correlation with the depth you have dug down. At first, you had purely seen the hatch in the floor of the shed area, as a portal to a potential escape route from the summerhouse; a back door, if you like. Now, however, as you have widened and deepened the pit beneath the hatch, you are struck by more ambitious schemes. It is feeling more secure, which has allowed you to expand your horizons. The chain on the front door is affording you a better night's sleep, and you are able to spend much longer now on your diggings each day, secure in the knowledge that no one can enter the summerhouse unannounced and take you by surprise. Not that your greater activity hasn't brought its own set of new logistical problems, chief amongst which is the disposal of all the excess soil from your pit in the floor.

Should you have been familiar with all those previously mentioned British cultural icons—like Robin Hood, the Great Train Robbery, and Peter Rabbit—you would surely also have been familiar with the perennial Christmas Day classic afternoon movie, *The Great Escape*. But you are not, and you are not. However, should you have been, it would have been inevitable that the idea to conceal the soil in specially adapted pouches made from old socks, which you attached to the inside of your trouser legs, and from which you could surreptitiously control the gradual dispersal of the soil from the bottom of your trousers as you walked around, would have occurred to you at some point in time. Similarly, if you had ever watched *The Great Escape*, it would have been an even bet that you would have also watched *The Wooden Horse* and, if that had been the case, possibilities of disposing of your excess soil via the expedient of a large gymnastic vaulting box might also have crossed your mind. But you have not, and you have not, and it has not. It is something to be thankful that you are free of all these jingoistic and unpractical distractions and, instead, you have fallen back on the unpretentious instrument of a bucket and trowel, and the simple concealment of the night. Nevertheless, it is not an easy procedure. You are still mindful of all the nocturnal hazards, which could still threaten your well-being: the pissing policeman; the copulating couple; the random wino. You have tried to spread your load of soil no euphemism intended, if any taken—across as many different allotment plots as it has been possible, although some element of proximity has inevitably guided your choice, and so your tall, fair-haired neighbour has probably received a greater share of the detritus from your excavations than any other allotment owner, not that you think he will notice; he definitely falls into the category of weekend gardener, rather than dedicated horticulturalist. Anyway, most allotment aficionados would be pleased to receive an extra bucketful of topsoil; it is the kind of thing that they could be expected to pay good money for at the local garden centre. It is perhaps a slightly different proposition now that you have struck more stones; even so, you are not to know if there might not be some would-be rockery builders amongst your compatriots. It somewhat eases the back-breaking task of shifting shit loads of soil by holding onto the belief that you might be doing someone else a good turn.

Chapter Fourteen

A Day at the Football

The tall, fair-haired man, minus his quilted green gilet, has had a busy morning digging. He is energetic, but unfocussed. Should you wish to be critical of him. You have started to become familiar with his timetable; it is as well established as your own one. Even observing him now, unconsciously, you are beginning to prepare for his departure; the locking of his door, the return and rechecking that the door is really locked, and then he is gone, you know not where. Today, though, has not conformed entirely to type. By your reckoning, he is rather late; his own frequent glances at his own watch would confirm that he is perhaps thinking the same thought. And he has been doing something odd. After completing his digging, and after stowing his spade away in his shed, he emerged again with a small plastic box, not dissimilar to one of the Tupperware containers that you have in your kitchen area, which used to contain sugar and that still contains tea bags—in fact, almost identical, now that you look closer—and from this container he had picked out several small, hard objects—they looked like stones, from your distant viewpoint—which he proceeded to place on top of the earth, close to the front step of his shed. He took some pains to place these objects, standing back occasionally to admire his handiwork, as though the pattern of the arrangement was important to him. It is something for you to check out more closely, once he has gone.

Since you took over residency of the summerhouse, the tall, fair-haired man is the closest thing to a new friend that you have made. Admittedly, he doesn't know of your existence—will never know, if you remain lucky—and you know next to nothing about him—not his name; his occupation; where he lives—but the simple activity of watching his virtuous toil sparks a warm, sentimental emotion within you, which you have extended to include the man himself. You no longer think of the acquisition of the green gilet as a theft; it is more a gift; it is what the tall, fair-haired man would have wanted you to have should he have known you were there.

Seclusion is the flipside of the security that the summerhouse has brought you. For the period of time when you had been living rough on the streets, there had been a large community of similarly-placed individuals and, although you would not have gone as far as to say that any of the people you had encountered had become friends—a few actively becoming enemies instead—there had been a collective feeling of shared humanity, which fulfilled some primeval need. You are safer now, but you are also more alone. Most of the time you have spent in the summerhouse you have managed to keep sufficiently busy not to suffer from any great feelings of loneliness but, just occasionally, you recall the world you have lost, one rich with family and friends; shared laughter; shared sadnesses.

It is the resolution of a second to decide to follow the tall, fair-haired man. You have no intention of introducing yourself; no desire to speak to him, but you have a sudden, over-riding desire to know something about him above and beyond that of his allotment existence. Somehow the shared activity draws you closer together, too, even though on his part he is entirely oblivious to taking part. As a target, the tall, fair-haired man is an easy mark. His height makes him stand out from the crowd; his lack of suspicion renders you practically invisible. You watch for him to lock the door of his summerhouse, wait for him to return and recheck the lock, and only then do you fix the padlock on the door of the summerhouse and begin your pursuit; keeping your distance; walking down a parallel path through the allotment to the one, which he is following; never failing to let him entirely disappear from your sight. There is something childishly pleasurable about the activity; it reminds you of games you had played with friends around your old neighbourhood when you had been a kid; something hauntingly adult, too, bringing to mind the all-too-real challenges of hide-and-seek when you had sought to evade opposition troops in the wrecked shell of your home town. Also, there is something primordial about it: an animalistic hunt; the stalker and its prey. In the past you had always been the prey; now you felt what it was to be the stalker.

The tall, fair-haired man makes directly for the main gate of the allotments. He has a long, purposeful stride, and he walks with a strong, straight back, chest out, shoulders back; almost military in his bearing. There is an air of confidence about him, which belies his OCD trait of rechecking the lock. Someone who is slow to make a decision but who, once decided, is implacable in seeing it through. That is your assessment, for what it's worth.

See, you feel as though you are one step closer to knowing him already.

At the gates, he turns left; no hesitation, and proceeds to walk down Bishop's Avenue in the direction of the river. You hurry slightly in order to close the distance between the two of you since the street is crowded with people. For a moment, you pause to wonder why. You have never seen it so busy before. Then it strikes you. The football. It must be a match day. The crowds are predominately men; mainly wearing colours of white and black. There is a background noise of chattering voices; dozens of separate conversations, all focussed on one single theme. You wonder if the tall, fair-haired man is going to the football. He doesn't seem the type. Or, does he? You don't really know. You are only a dozen paces behind him now, but in the melee of bodies, you are invisible. In contrast, he remains as obvious as a lighthouse amidst the piebald sea.

At the corner of the road, he turns right, cutting through Bishops Park; so, the river is not his objective; could still be the football; might just as possibly be the Bishops Park public toilets. No, you pass the toilets—straight back, chest out, shoulders back––and carry straight on into Stevenage Road. More people filter into your stream of humanity from Bishop's Park Road, having the effect of slowing the overall flow, smoothing out the individual eddies, unifying the forward movement. You surmise that the football must be the tall, fair-haired man's objective after all; there are alternative routes he could have taken, which would have been quicker if he had wanted to avoid this crowd; although, perhaps once he had come to this realisation it was already too late—someone slow to make a decision, you remind yourself—and he is now caught in the surge; helpless flotsam, like yourself.

You find yourself squeezed up against the railings, which border Bishops Park; attempt to edge towards the road, deeper into the crowd of bodies. Pavement and roadway have become one, engulfed by the unstoppable tide. You can still see the tall, fair-haired man ahead of you, but he is further away now; his height and demeanour have been more successful at negotiating a passage through the crowds than your cowering insignificance. Ahead, you can see the end-on view of an ugly white football stand—a notice on the gates states that it is the 'Putney End'—and a row of numbered, narrow black doors, stark against a long, red-brick wall, which look rather like toilet cubicles, but which are clearly the turnstiles to the stadium. Further on still is the façade of an elegant, three-storey brick building with Dutch gables on the roof, which looks rather like a railway station, but which proudly proclaims itself 'The Fulham Football Club' in big white letters against a black background. A portion of the crowd has peeled off, but the section that you are caught in surges forward with renewed energy, bringing you hard up against a cylindrical brick and white stone plinth. It is an unmoveable obstruction around which the crowd diverges to left and right. You cling to it like a shipwrecked sailor to a life-raft, gratefully accepting the sanctuary of its protection in order to momentarily extract you from the relentless tide of bodies.

For the first time, you look up. On top of the plinth, is the bronze statue of a footballer, hands on hips, one foot firmly planted on top of a football, a determined expression beneath a sculptural quiff of hair. Engraved letters in the stone base declare it to be Johnny Haynes, The Maestro Captain of England and Fulham FC. You run your forefinger along the engraving, tracing out the sharp edges of the big capitals. Johnny Haynes. Like Robin Hood, and the Great Train Robbery, and Peter Rabbit, and *The Great Escape*, you had never heard of him. If ever there was the need for a helpful blue information plaque, it was now.

Digression Fourteen.One
Craven Cottage

Craven Cottage is the name of the stadium of Fulham Football Club. The current stadium dates from 1894, but the original Craven Cottage was built in 1780 by William Craven, the sixth Baron Craven as a hunting lodge. It was a pretty thatched, two-storey building, with a gable roof, tall chimneys, and overgrown by climbing plants, surrounded by gardens and woodland, all within the grounds of the Bishop's Palace. The cottage became the home of the writer and politician Edward Bulwer-Lytton, but was destroyed by fire in 1888.

The distinctive pavilion, which is known as the 'Cottage', and which fills the northeast corner of the ground between the Putney End and the Johnny Haynes Stand was built by Scottish architect Archibald Leitch in 1905.

Fulham Football Club itself was founded in 1879, as the Fulham St Andrews Church Football Club, and despite having played in all four professional divisions of the English football league system, they are yet to win a major trophy. Should you have been able to discover this solitary heart-wrenching fact from the non-existent blue information plaque, your heart would have warmed to them. You have always favoured backing the underdog. Nevertheless, you feel a certain kinship to them simply because they are now your nearest, neighbouring team.

Despite having many big-name players donning the traditional black and white strip over the years, such as George Best, Rodney Marsh and Dimitar Berbatov, Fulham's most famous son is Johnny Haynes, who made 594 appearances for Fulham between 1952 and 1970, scoring 146 goals.

The statue to Johnny Haynes was made by sculptor Douglas Jennings, and was erected outside the ground in 2008. More controversially, a statue to the pop singer Michael Jackson was erected inside the ground by then owner Mohamed Al-Fayed in 2011, despite the fact that Jackson was only ever known to once visit the ground to watch Fulham beat Wigan Athletic by two goals to nil in 1999. The statue did not survive redevelopment plans in 2013, and was subsequently moved to the National Football Museum.

• • •

You catch a final glimpse of the tall, fair-haired man in the crowds at the far end of the stadium, but whether he entered the ground via the turnstiles at the Hammersmith End or carried on down Stevenage Road you are unable to tell.

You begin to retrace your steps back to the allotments. Most of the crowd have now taken their seats in the stadium, and the surrounding street has emptied, except for a line of uniformed police officers, and two mounted constables on horseback. Instinctively, you avert your eyes and attempt to shy away from these representatives of authority, but you are not given so much as a second glance. Alfred Wurgihurt is invisible to the scrutiny of the forces of law and order.

Back home, before you enter the summerhouse, you examine the ground in front of the shed belonging to the tall, fair-haired man to see what it was that he had been laying on the ground. Arranged in a neat ornamental pattern, half-pressed into the brown top soil are eight small fossil ammonites, coiled and cold. You pick up one, weigh it in your hand, and then put it in your pocket. You smooth over the disturbed earth, and subtly rearrange the other ammonites so that the gap is not conspicuous. On the chart of thefts, it does not even rate a mention.

Chapter Fifteen

The Vegetable Garden

As the seasons change so, too, does your diet. With the last frosts of winter behind you, increasingly there is a greater variety of vegetables—and even some fruit now—being grown on the various plots across the allotment. There are cabbages and onions, carrots, spinach, some garlic to add flavour, and you have a particular eye on an allotment in the far northeast corner, where you have seen the suspicion of a healthy crop of asparagus starting to emerge. With careful plundering, you think that you will be able to extract a few spears each day without the loss being too evident. One allotment is overgrown with a plant with big, dark green leaves and bright, bright red stalks, which you do not recognise from your homeland. It looks like it should be tasty, but you have sampled both the leaves and the stalks raw, and also cooked, and you cannot yet decide whether it is edible or not. On the whole, you think it is something best left well alone. At home now, you would have been enjoying oranges, plucked directly from the trees, which used to grow outside your old house, but you know that they don't grow in this cold land. It is not the only thing that you miss, but it is a good metaphor for all that you have lost, and less emotional demanding than considering a never-ending roll-call of names and relationships and faces.

The manky fox is still a regular visitor, his night-time barks often bringing you to the window of the summerhouse to stare out into the impenetrable blackness, but the two frolicking cubs have long gone. The slender, white cat continues to be an occasional ghost but, thankfully, she no longer prefers your allotment for her litter tray; perhaps the presence of Alfred Wurgihurt's decaying corpse six foot under is subliminally deterring her. The 'copper' still makes his nightly rounds but, on the whole, you have now come to consider him in his proper lawful role as protector of your property, rather than anyone that you have reason to fear.

All things considered, everything in your garden is fairly rosy.

Digression Fifteen.One

The Poison Garden

The planting of poisonous plants and shrubs in gardens, both unofficial and official, has a long history from the ancient Greeks to monastic medicinal gardens in medieval Europe, but the first recognised poison garden was probably that of the *Orto Botanico di Padova*, much venerated by herbalists, and frequented by the influential Medici family. The fame of this unusual horticultural attraction spread across Europe, and it was not long before the green fingered bishops at Fulham Palace decide that a poison garden would add kudos to their own illustrious grounds. A site close to the river, in the southeast corner of the gardens was chosen, and it was not long before the distinctive purple stars of deadly nightshade (*Atropa belladonna*); the delicate hoods of Wolf's-bane (*Aconitum);* the brilliant pink bells of Foxglove (*Digitalis*); and the pale green spathes of Cuckoo-pint (*Arum maculatum*) found a safe sanctuary to root amidst the holy enclaves, free from persecution and prejudice. Indeed, for several summers, the poison garden was the must-see attraction of the palace; a *de rigueur* stopping off point for visitors to the palace.

The Danish delegation, which attended Elizabeth's banquet in 1601 was no exception to this rule, and the chief gardener at the time considered it an honour to be able to escort such an important group of noblemen around what he had come to consider as his private garden. He was knowledgeable on the subject of the plants and shrubs, having sourced many of them himself from more distant parts of the country and was keen to stress their medicinal qualities but, as was common amongst most visitors to the garden, all that anyone really wanted to know was which of the plants was the deadliest; how swiftly death could occur; and what kind of gruesome and graphic symptoms would ensue. Resigned to play along to his audience, the head gardener recounted several tales of hideous poisonings, both true and imaginary; recited rumoured accounts of the notorious Medici family's various murderous exploits, which had reached the Palace's notice from Mediterranean Europe; and introduced each new species of plant with an element of grand theatrical melodrama, which would not have been out of place amidst the performances of the Lord Chamberlain's Men on the stage of the Globe Theatre.

At the rear of the delegation of diplomats, one young Dane dawdled, perceptively bored by proceedings. He could neither speak nor understand a single word of English, and he had found both the journey, the meal, the company, and now this long-winded, guided tour around the cold and windy Palace grounds, unspeakably boring. So, it was unseen by the rest of the company that he allowed a curious hand to languidly trail across the dark, purple hooded flowers, which were growing so invitingly at his fingertips; unnoticed that he licked fingers suddenly sticky with resin; and unobserved that he began to fall behind the rest of the group.

It was not until several hours later that he was discovered missing. He was still in the poison garden, but he was no longer admiring the beguiling mauve plants. Death had not been instantaneous, but that had been no mercy. He would first have experienced a numbness to the face, then a weakness in his limbs. By the time he was in the grip of chest palpitations and vomiting, he was already too weak to cry out.

Chapter Sixteen

Friends and Followers

The tall, fair-haired man became a less frequent weekend visitor to the neighbouring allotment, and then suddenly he was gone, never to return. You never did follow him again, nor find out anything more about his life beyond the allotment walls. However, you did follow several other people. It had become something of a game for you. Often when you were bored; usually when you were feeling lonely, you would attach yourself to a random stranger and follow them. Except it is not entirely true to say that your choice was random; a degree of conscious selection took place.

For example, it was rare that you started your hunt within the allotment itself. To some degree, this was based on a process of trial and error. Twice you had attempted to follow a fellow allotment owner, only for it to prove to be a false start. On the first occasion, the man had simply been admiring a neighbouring gardener's lettuces, and the second time, your chosen target had only gone as far as the communal trading hut to pick up a big bag of compost. Already, you are conscious of the language with which you describe your game, and you do not wish to give the wrong impression. Both 'hunt' and 'target' make your activity sound altogether predatory, which is the last thing you have in mind. Similarly, 'stalk' has negative connotations, but you cannot think of another word, which more accurately describes this occupation, because 'follow' sounds a little too passive; it doesn't give you sufficient credit for the act of seeing whilst remaining unseen.

Outside of the allotments, the pursuit—a better word; evoking both the element of skill and the element of fun—is more unpredictable. That is where it is important to be selective. For starters, you never follow women. Culturally, morally, socially: it is wrong on so many levels. Also, pragmatically, you are still acutely aware of your own 'uncertain' status in the eyes of the law and following a woman seems like a quick way to draw unwelcome attention on yourself. If you are being entirely honest, too, you must also admit to a certain amount of gender stereotyping in your decision; you can't altogether break historic ties to a predominately machismo culture that prejudices you to make the assumption that to follow a woman would only lead you to either a shop or a café. With men, it is different. You just never know where the pursuit will take you. You have followed business men to Hammersmith Station; lunching builders to the pub; a young, blonde tourist to a backpacker's hostel close to Holland Park; even a middle-aged clergyman across the bridge and on a long walk to the centre of Wimbledon Common, although, in hindsight, you wonder whether he may have spotted you early-doors and was actually luring you to an assignation of his own interpretation; a neat prey turned predator reversal. Never once have you actually spoken to any of the people you have followed. Why would you? What have you got to say? The story of the recent history of your homeland; the wars and the injustices; of how your own family have all been either killed or displaced such that you have no idea how to contact them;

a tale of flight and escape: bitter experience has taught you that no one wants to hear any of that. You suppose that you could talk about your new life; about your new identity as Alfred Wurgihurt; about your plans for the summerhouse; about the crops that you hope to grow on your allotment at some time in the future. Except knowledge of human psychology warns you that no one wants to hear that either. Most people only want to listen to talk about themselves and, since all the people whom you have followed are complete strangers to you, you have no means of entering into the conversation.

It may sound a little lonely your existence; even a little bit nihilistic your philosophy. But is it any less remote than the world of social media? The friends and the followers. The three hundred digital acquaintances who pass as friends; the rag-tag collection of strangers whom you follow but whose opinions you are swift to scroll over and never listen to. On the whole, you prefer your own collection of new friends. The businessman at Hammersmith, the builders in the pub, the backpacker on his Gap Year. You may never get to know any of their names, but at least they are real, tangible entities. Even the dodgy vicar on the common. Especially the dodgy vicar on the common.

Chapter Seventeen

Three-fingers Returns

You could never have made a wiser investment than the £8.59 you spent in Putney Hardware for a standard metallic door chain. You had had no prior warning that a visitor to the summerhouse was imminent; this time he did not introduce himself with a loudly-voiced conversation with your neighbour; no, he was there, standing immediately outside, rattling the front door to the summerhouse before you had the first inkling of his approach. As it was, the door opened several inches but the chain halted your intruder in his tracks; permitted you a vital few seconds of time to spring into action, quite literally; you took one deft leap from the position where you had been reclining on the old *chaise longue* to conceal yourself beneath the small, wooden table beneath the window. It was a position from which you could not be observed even by someone putting their eye right up to the crack in the doorway, but from where you could keep a lookout on the entrance. Your military training in your homeland had taught you many similar tricks; covering your lines of defence; securing the best position for attack. Nevertheless, it was with a sense of palpable anxiety that you witnessed the continued incursion. You could feel a bead of sweat running down from your forehead, past the corner of your eye, and along the side of your nose. You wanted to wipe it away, but you did not dare move a muscle for fear that any sound would alert the invader to the fact that the summerhouse was occupied.

Without having to see his face, you recognised him from his fingers. You had seen them before; seen them in similar circumstances. Three lined and grubby fingers furled around the doorframe, the tips brown with nicotine and soil, the little finger on the right hand conspicuously missing.

"Alf?"

It is the same appeal that he had made on his previous visit. You recognise the voice; the accent; the timbre.

The three fingers momentarily disappear, and the door is violently rattled back and forth, but the chain holds. The voice is louder now; more urgent:

"Alf! Are you in there?"

The fingers are back at the door frame again. This time you can see that they are snaking forward, attempting to extend further through the narrow gap between the door and the jamb, their intention only too apparent: to attempt to dislodge the slider of the chain out of its latch. There is nothing that you can do other than to watch as the three gnarled digits squirm and slither, gradually inching their way along the links of the cool metal chain. You want to jump out from your place of hiding, throw yourself bodily against the door, crushing the repellent prying fingers in the process, but common sense—and a little bit of human decency—prevails; you know that you will be best served by remaining doggo.

There is the sound of cursing from outside the doorway; cursing, which you take to be a good sign. Your DIY security is proving impregnable to the first serious attempt at invasion; the gap between the door and the frame is not wide enough for three-fingers to insert his hand such that he can unhook the chain from the latch. You know that the door is not sufficiently strong to resist a determined shoulder-barge, but it appears that three-fingers is nervous to make such a drastic step: a sneaky trespass is one thing, but actual criminal damage is something else altogether.

There is a slight noise at the window directly above you. From your position beneath the table, you cannot see what is happening, but it does not take too great a leap of the imagination to picture three-fingers pressing his nose to the glass, his maimed hand shielding his eyes, attempting to peer into the dark recesses of the interior. You remain still, drawing in your legs and feet, so that they do not extend beyond the area, which the table-top conceals; find yourself holding your breath, although you know that such a slight sound could not be heard by someone standing outside. The tableau remains motionless for minutes; at least, it seems like minutes to you; in reality it is only a matter of a few seconds before you hear another curse from outside, and a bang, as of a fist striking glass, but not hard enough to break it; just the final frustrated action of a raider repelled.

From your place of concealment, you count to ten. Slowly, and deliberately; permitting your heart-rate the chance to return to normal; allowing your unwelcome visitor the opportunity to fully vacate your territory. Cautiously, you inch yourself out backwards from beneath the table; almost scared to look up at the window in case the darkly-lined face you have pictured in imagination is still there, staring directly in at you. But there is no one.

You do not like this sensation of being made to feel an alien in your own home. Hiding beneath tables and skulking in the shadows: it is an insult to your self-respect and pride. After the relief of non-discovery, you experience a wave of anger towards the man who has provoked these emotions in you; who has so summarily brought you to this position of humiliation. Almost without thinking, you make a move to follow the would-be intruder. You want to confront him; frighten him; invoke the same undignified reactions in him that he has brought on you. You slip the chain from the latch in easy conscious irony of the struggles of your adversary; shut the front door behind you, but don't bother to lock it, in the fever of your pursuit. Neither Three-fingers, nor anyone else is in sight across the green vista of the allotments, but you are not deterred: he has only a single line of retreat; if you hurry, you can cut him off.

You race along a narrow gravel path between allotment plots on either side of you. Normally, you would not risk drawing attention to yourself, but you are confident that there are sufficiently few people around such that your lapse in accepted behaviour will pass largely unnoticed. You cut behind a large see-through Polytunnel, full of new seedlings, and skip across three raised timber cold-frames as though they are hurdles in a steeplechase race. Even now, though, and despite your urgency, you are mindful of your fellow gardeners' labours. You avoid a potential shortcut across one allotment because it has been recently dug, and the soil turned and flattened with such Zen-like obvious care and attention that to plant your footprints across the perfectly even surface would be an act of vandalism akin to defiling a work of art. And you skirt another plot, because the chicane of raspberry canes provides an almost insurmountable barrier to your progress of Viet Cong ingenuity. However, you can see the exit to the allotments now and, on a path parallel to you, and just a little way ahead, the same slightly stooped figure, with tufty wisps of white hair emerging from a flat, checked cap who you had encountered during your early days in the summerhouse.

Now that your quarry is in sight, you are less swift to close the gap between you. Suddenly, it seems less important to effect a confrontation between the two of you, as it does to follow the man. Here is someone who had known the real Alfred Wurgihurt. Not for the first time, you wonder what was the relationship between the two men? Instinctively, you fall into the pattern of your recent game. Three-fingers is simply another interested party to follow; to find out where he leads you; to piece together fragments of a life from any clues you can gather along the way. Somehow, you do not think that you are likely to add Three-fingers to your list of 'friends', but he is a welcome 'follower'.

It does not take you very long tailing Three-fingers before you realise that you are on the trail of a very different kind of adversary than most of your normal targets. Where someone like the tall, fair haired man had walked along apparently oblivious to his surroundings, Three-fingers displays all the nervous traits of a hunted criminal, constantly on the lookout for potential trouble.

Where the tall, fair haired man had never once so much as glanced behind him, Three-fingers constantly casts anxious looks backwards over the ground he has just trod, as though he is someone anticipating pursuit. All things considered, it made the chase altogether more interesting, and surprisingly more invigorating. For once, you were able to deploy some of your skills of concealment; of urban camouflage; challenge yourself in a way that other occasions following people had not done.

Initially, it had looked as though Three-fingers was going to cross the bridge. From outside the allotments, he had taken the route down to the river, then up the stairs next to the big church, where he had turned right onto the main carriageway, which crosses the bridge itself. He had paused briefly in the bus shelter, made as though he was consulting the timetable, and then had rapidly retraced his steps, so that suddenly he was coming directly towards you. You were not alarmed. You maintained an appearance of affected nonchalance, allowing him to pass you without so much as an exchanged glance. You continued to walk on for several steps, pausing yourself at the bus shelter, from where you were able to turn and observe your quarry. He was still in sight, walking away from you now at some considerable pace; a determined stride as though he had some definite purpose in mind. You were obliged to jog briefly in order to make up some of your lost ground. However, the main road was busy both with traffic and pedestrians and you did not think that your hurrying would be particularly noticed.

Ahead of you, Three-fingers had now crossed the main road, skipping through the flow of cars with a practised urban familiarity, which belied his apparent years, and had taken a right turning, the name of which you saw was New King's Road when you were close enough to read the street sign. There were fewer people now, and you allowed a larger gap to develop between the two of you. Another fork in the road, and Three-fingers once again took the right-hand one, moving to pass beneath the green, metal railway bridge, which looked like a giant freight container, out of place beside its brick supports, but, then again, he double-backed, retraced his steps, and took the left-hand junction instead. If anything, he was walking even faster. He held one hand to his cap, as though scared that it might blow off. Beneath another narrow railway bridge, past a chi-chi parade of local shops until, suddenly, on the right-hand side a small green park appeared. He stopped beside a rack of bicycles for hire, bent over as though he was attempting to catch his breath, and then took several purposeful steps back towards you, deliberately blocking your path.

"What's your game, then?"

You pretended to ignore the words, stepping to one side as though to pass him, but he moved to block you again.

"You hear me? What's your game following me?"

His old, lined face was contorted with anger; the words spat out with a dangerous venom.

You turned around; tried to walk away from him, back the way you had come, but you had only taken a couple of steps when you felt his hand on your shoulder, halting you; the three obscene fingers pressing hard into your collar with an urgent insistence.

"Don't walk away when I'm talking to you. I want to know what you think you're doing?"

You kick backwards, your shoe striking his shin. As you feel his hand release your shoulder, you break into a run. You hear a torrent of abuse following you along the road, but you don't look back. You know that you have the beating of him in a straight foot race. It is not until you are back to the parade of shops that you dare to slow you speed and, when you look back towards the small park, Three-fingers is no longer anywhere in sight.

You deliberately take a circuitous route back to the allotments, designed to frustrate any possible pursuit. Now it is your turn to feel the hunted, not the hunter. It is not a nice feeling. It is one that you remember only too well from old, back in your homeland. It is with a sense of palpable relief that you regain the sanctuary of the summerhouse. You reattach the chain across the front door, put the kettle on to make a cup of tea, and sit down heavily on the *chaise longue*, giving yourself time to settle your breathing. For some reason, you think of Alfred Wurgihurt's dirty tea cup. It still remains unwashed, in the small recessed cupboard beneath the sink where you stashed it away on the first day that you had discovered the summerhouse. You think of Three-fingers, too. Perhaps his visit was nothing more sinister than an attempt to return the container of sugar he had borrowed? Although, for some reason, you don't think so.

Chapter Eighteen
Breakthrough

You are conscious that the time you have spent following strangers has become a distraction from your main task, which is enlarging the hole beneath the hatch in your shed. The fleeting pursuit of companionship has diverted your mind from more creditable goals. You like to think of yourself as someone who is conscientious, but you know that you can become quickly distracted. It is not that you are allergic to hard work—quite the opposite; you relish a task that exercises both your mind and body––it has simply been the case that the more comfortable you have become in the summerhouse, the less inclination you have had to construct the tunnel, the original purpose of which was to form a means of exit from the rear of the building. However, the recent visit by Three-fingers has reaffirmed the need of such an escape route, and has reinvigorated your motivation for the task. Returning to the job, you can't understand why you abandoned the project when you appeared so close to a breakthrough.

The hole is much larger than you remembered it. Something over twelve feet deep, and with a sizeable floor area, such that there is space at the bottom to stand and manoeuvre. You had constructed a wooden ladder, which runs from the base of the pit to a point a couple of feet below the rim, to effect ease of exit and entry. The wood for the ladder you had stolen—the activity is becoming so second nature to you now that you scarcely update your graph of thieving—from a fellow allotment owner. It was not a very communal spirited act, but sometimes needs take precedence over good manners. And, if nothing else, it justified the expense of having a policeman patrol each night. The wood had evidently been intended to be used to build an ornamental trellis, but it was a gift, which you would have been foolish to ignore. Alfred Wurgihurt had supplied the necessary saw, nails and hammer to complete the construction, which you had worked on in the shed for several nights, muffling the sound of the actual hammering with a wodge—not a precise technical term—of old material. The first time you had used the ladder, you had been nervous that the rungs would not take your weight, but you should have had more confidence in your abilities, and the construction has held firm. Once an engineer, always an engineer.

And then you had simply upped tools; stopped work, leaving the mysterious, subterranean barrier of bricks unbreached; your carefully selected stone chisel unsullied and unused. Except, no longer. Standing at the bottom of the pit, body tensed, legs braced, a fierce light playing on the wall of bricks from your handy Maglite, you angled your chisel at a point where two of the narrow bricks met, and struck the shaft end a purposeful blow with your hammer. There was a satisfying splintering of masonry, a shower of brick dust, and, more encouraging to your ears, an unmistakeable hollow ring, which suggested that there might be some kind of recess beyond the brick wall. That would be the Grail in your mind: to discover an opening, which might possibly circumvent the necessity of further extensive and time-consuming excavation work.

A small cavity had opened up where you had made your first incursion, and you renewed your efforts against this point of weakness. Shards of brick steadily chipped away, some forming dangerous missiles, which you had no protection against. A pair of goggles would have been a sensible additional purchase at Putney Hardware, but it is always easy to be wise after the event. You did take the precaution of wrapping one of your older shirts around your face like a *keffiyeh*, because the dust in the confined space of the shaft was becoming stifling, and you had found yourself beginning to choke. It was not much assistance, but it was better than nothing.

Beyond the bricks, you could still see nothing. Not a chink of light shone through the small gap you had made, and progress was slow attempting to widen the cavity. You stuck a finger optimistically into the hole, but it was impossible to tell what lay beyond. You concentrated your attack on the joins between a section of four interlinked bricks, in the belief that if you could loosen the foundations of these blocks sufficiently, it might be possible to remove the entire section in one go. It was painstaking work. You had quickly discovered that brute force was no solution to the problem. All that that had achieved had been a pain in your shoulder and a sharp corner of flying brick striking you close to the corner of your eye, resulting in a thin, but persistent trickle of blood, running down the side of your nose. A calculated, more systematic assault on the wall was altogether more profitable; locating the points of weakness; angling your chisel to optimum advantage; limiting your hammer strokes for maximum effect.

It happened all at once. One sharp tap on the end of the chisel and, suddenly, the section of four bricks, which you had been attempting to loosen, slid backwards in one conjoined block for the distance of about an inch. It did not sound like much, but what it represented was huge. There must be a hollow space beyond the wall. It was only the matter of a few more minutes' work before you had pushed the bricks completely through the wall, hearing them fall with a satisfying thud on the other side. You were left with a hole, which was wide enough for you to put your hand through. For some inexplicable reason, the prospect rather alarmed you. You had no idea what lay on the other side of the opening. You were suddenly filled with horrifying visions of strange, supernatural, subterranean creatures grasping your hand from the other side of the abyss; of being pulled into a void from which there was no return. It was superstitious nonsense, but you could not entirely dispel the powerful image from your mind. Common sense came to your rescue. Rather than attempt to grope wildly about in the dark, you realised that you had a purpose-built tool at hand to help you. Shining your torch through the small, uneven gap you had created in the wall, so that you could clearly see what lay in the space beyond, brought with it both illumination but, also, a greater sense of mystery.

Digression Eighteen.One

A Secret Internment

It would be accurate to say that there was something of a shit storm occuring amidst the party of diplomats attending Elizabeth's banquet at the Bishop's Palace in 1601. But isn't that so often the way with diplomacy? It looks as though everything is going so well and, then, something entirely unexpected, which it would have been impossible to predict beforehand, comes out of leftfield to knock all the good work into a cocked hat.

The body of the young Danish clerk had been discovered a short while earlier. It did not have to take a keen herbalist to work out what had happened; the rictus of frozen anguish, which was writ large across the fair-haired youth's innocent face and the unnatural, contorted aspect of his limbs were enough to convict the purple flowers with their attractive bells and peculiarly hand-shaped leaves without recourse to any expert witnesses. As if resigned to their own guilt, the deadly plants hadn't even bothered to vacate the scene of the crime; instead, billowing over the corpse of the young man, their heads bowed like a row of grief-stricken mourners lining the path of a funereal cortège.

It had been a party of fairly low-ranking officials who had actually made the discovery of the body; two from the English delegation; one from the visiting Danes. There was considerable confusion what they should do next. It was imperative that Elizabeth should know nothing of the fatality. That was the number one consideration. Nor the Danish ambassador, for that matter. Nothing could be gained by his knowledge. Beyond that, it was decided that it would be necessary to bump the decision making one pay grade higher. Two noble personnel, one a high-ranking English clergyman, one a courtier to the Danish court, were surreptitiously consulted, and soon joined the group of worried individuals standing in the poison garden of Fulham Palace amidst the lethal blossoms and the setting sun. At stake was a lucrative trade agreement between the two countries; a normalisation of diplomatic relations, which had been allowed to become frayed. The discussions had so far proved successful, but everyone knew that Elizabethan diplomacy was like walking a tightrope between success and failure; there must be no late wobbles to potentially upset proceedings.

It was decided that the body would be hidden. Hidden somewhere that it would never be discovered. The English contingent would undertake the gruesome task of internment; whilst, the Danes would spin a story of the young man having last been seen rather the worse the wear for drink; presumably sleeping it off somewhere discrete. Drunk and dishonour a more palatable dish than death.

In the end, it was left to the most junior member of the English delegation to take care of the body. He enlisted the help of two gardeners from the Palace grounds and a large, wooden wheelbarrow in order to move the corpse. They knew just the place. A former Bishop had been much struck by the grottos he had witnessed in the village of Matera, during a visit on the invitation of a nobleman from the House of Aragon, so much so that, upon returning home, he had attempted to duplicate one of the structures in an obscure corner of the Palace grounds. The artificial cave duly constructed had proved little more than a five-minute wonder, and the folly had quickly fallen into neglect, its entrance overgrown by weeds, its existence now known only to a select few. As a final resting place for the unfortunate Danish clerk, it had the advantage of obscurity and the benefit of dignity. For the two gardeners, transporting the corpse was no more strenuous than carting a load of manure. Untroubled by either politics or conscience, they were perfectly content to carry out their latest assignment without any questions asked, particularly when a couple of groats had exchanged hands to smooth over any potential misunderstandings. The young English diplomat was more worried. He was more acutely aware of the consequences of failure. He, also, possessed something of an imagination and, as he oversaw the concealment of the body of his Danish counterpart in a dark and damp corner of the underground chamber, he could picture their situations being reversed; could believe how his own body might one day be stretched out, unmourned and unnoticed, in an anonymous corner of some distant field in Denmark.

The gardeners had completed their task—manual labour, nothing more, nothing less—and had retreated, leaving the young Englishman alone with the corpse. He felt as though he should say a few words of piety, but he was a good Reformationist, and nothing meaningful came to him. He stooped over the body; its eyes were wide and staring; the least he could do would be to close them; his attention was taken by a large ring on the dead man's finger. Instinctively, he glanced around him before he slipped the ring from the young Dane's hand; it was as though he had already committed himself to a particular course of action. He tossed the ring into the air; caught it again; felt its weight. It was heavy. Silver, without a doubt. Worth a bit. A waste to leave it on a corpse. There was an unusual inscription on the metal. Strange symbols, unfamiliar to the Englishman. Letters formed of harsh straight lines and crisp, well defined corners. Melted down, the symbols would be lost. Melted down, nobody would know. He returned the ring to the Dane's finger.

He would know.

• • •

It looked like a cave. Admittedly, your torch did not illuminate a very wide expanse but, from the little that you could see, it looked like a cave. A cave beneath the summerhouse. That was rather odd. Odd, but interesting. It was going to be necessary to greatly widen the hole you had formed in order to properly explore any further. It was already getting quite late. It was the task for another day.

Chapter Nineteen

Rent

You woke up to discover a small envelope pushed under the door of the summerhouse. It must have been delivered very early. You hadn't heard any noise from the dawn postman. There was no name on the front of the envelope, simply the plot number of your allotment.

Inside was a demand for money. Not a threatening one. Not the kind of heavy-handed blackmail, which your tenuous occupancy potentially exposed you to, but a simply stated IOU. Apparently, it was time to pay the annual subscription for the allotment to the Fulham Palace Meadows Allotment Association. Sixty quid. In the grand scheme of things, it was not a lot. Very modest, in fact. You would be very hard pressed to find a cheaper rent in such a desirable postcode. Except, of course, you didn't have the readies. Since your outlay on the standard metallic door chain, pocket-sized Maglite, and a large stone chisel suitable for cutting bricks, not to mention your splurge on the meal out, you were skint. Brassic. Possessed only a handful of coppers to show for your name. After all the hard work that you had put into the summerhouse, it seemed inconceivable that you might possibly be evicted for the sake of sixty quid. You needed a quick, money-making idea.

Some of your fellow allotment owners sold their produce at the communal shop. It was an activity, which was never going to produce any overnight millionaires, but it appeared to bring in a steady trickle of income for the gardeners who could be prepared to sit behind a counter of spring onions and Little Gem lettuce for several hours on end. The problem was that your own allotment had proved to be rather a sterile patch since your occupancy—you only ever claimed to be an engineer, never a gardener—and, more crucially, you could not risk the exposure of being seen in front of people who might know the real Alfred Wurgihurt. There would be questions asked.

You could go back to begging on the streets. Spend the days out collecting money; come back and spend the nights in the comfort of the summerhouse. It was an occupation, which had provided you with some cash in the past. However, begging was something of a lottery. Good days and bad days. Some of your fellow knights-of-the-street had been experts at the job; had known exactly the right pitches; had known to be at the right places at the right times—pubs and clubs closing hours; train station commuter rush hours—had been capable of exhibiting just the right balance of humour and pathos and earnestness. You had never been that successful. You liked to put it down to being more honest. Sometimes, in your most pessimistic moments, you blamed your lack of success on the fact that you were a foreigner. The fact was you had yet to reach the necessary degree of desperation. You had been fortunate enough to never lose your belief that your time living on the streets was only a period of transition; that better things would be around the corner. You had been even more fortunate to find your hopes realised in the discovery of the summerhouse. You weren't prepared to lose everything you had gained for the sake of a measly sixty nicker, but nor were you prepared to beg again in order to achieve it. There must be other ways.

Thieving was an invidious profession. Invidious because it had crept up and become almost second nature to you without you even being aware of it. You are conscious that the parameters of your personal scale of thefts have shifted significantly during the past few months such that crimes, which before you would have deemed noteworthy offences, now no longer even register. In this affluent neighbourhood of London, you would be fairly confident that a quick mugging of practically any random passer-by would net you the necessary dosh to pay off your landlord's demand, plus leave you with a little left over for a few luxuries—perhaps buy those goggles to protect your eyes for when you return to excavating the basement—but some residual vestige of morality prevents you from venturing any further in that direction. At heart, you are a good man, even if you have to keep saying it to remind yourself of the fact.

In the past, who have you turned to when you have required help? Long, long ago, it would have been your parents. The providers of more than you can ever know; sadly, both long dead. You have often—often? Sometimes—turned to religion. Similar to begging, though, religion is something of an uncertain pursuit. Good days and bad days again. And, unlike begging, the insertion of a little skill into the equation never seems to greatly improve the odds. More recently, you have relied on one particular individual. Alfred Wurgihurt. So far, he has never let you down when you have needed him most. Once again, you are confident that he will provide in your hour of need. In Alfred Wurgihurt you trust.

Chapter Twenty

The Legacy of Alfred Wurgihurt

It required another journey across the bridge in order to access Alfred Wurgihurt's bank. For some reason, you always regarded a journey across the bridge as something of a momentous occasion. You were still conscious of that process of transition. From fugitive to free man. For you, the south side of the bridge represented a world of possibilities; the north side, the reality of daily life, albeit a reality, which was improving every day. The north was your commonplace; the south a promised land of hope, as yet unfulfilled. And it was hope that you were banking on now. Alfred Wurgihurt's bank card had already delivered you from one sticky situation; you were hoping that it might prove its worth once again, now.

It was the first time that you had used a cashpoint machine in your new homeland. It was not as though they were any kind of scary tech that was unfamiliar to you—the design was pretty much universal across the globe—but, the fact is, you had always experienced a sense of trepidation when using one, even in your own country. Old-fashioned maybe but, when dealing with money, you had always preferred the shared intimacy of a face-to-face transaction. A thick wodge—still not a technical term—of greasy notes being exchanged between sweaty palms; there was an honesty there, somehow; or, if a dishonesty, a dishonesty, which had to be played out in plain sight. An electronic transfer between anonymous computer systems thousands of miles apart was so much more impersonal, whilst still presenting opportunities for many a slip 'twixt the cup and the lip.

You now knew Alfred Wurgihurt's PIN off by heart. There would be no slip-ups, like in the restaurant. Instinctively, you glanced around you to make sure that you were not being observed before you tapped in the four-digit code into the keypad. The list of options was longer than you expected. Some of the words were unfamiliar to you, however 'cash' stood out bold and clear. The 'amount' menu was equally obvious: you had a choice of £10; £20; £30; £50; £100; or £200. You only needed sixty quid, but you might as well try to withdraw a ton while you were at it. The extra cash would always come in handy. What the hell! Why not make it two hundred, since you were here? Before you had time to change your mind, you pressed the button. Was this stealing? Had your catalogue of thefts reached a new level of depravity? Or were you quite legitimately making a cash withdrawal from the bank account of Alfred Wurgihurt? And who's Alfred Wurgihurt? You're Alfred Wurgihurt!

Although, if you *are* Alfred Wurgihurt, you have absolutely no idea how much money Alfred Wurgihurt has in his personal current account. While you anxiously wait, and listen as the internal workings of the machine whirr and gurgle as it shuffles banknotes like a magician with a pack of cards, you ponder the alternative options, which the machine doesn't mention to you. Press 1: your card will be rejected. Press 2: your card will be confiscated. Press 3: a siren will start to sound; red flashing lights will start up; the doors of the bank will automatically slam shut; and a team of armed response officers will surround you and arrest you on the spot for the illegal withdrawal of funds from a dead man's account. In the event, none of these things happen. Instead, there is the slightest sound of mechanical activity and a neat bundle of crisp twenty-pound notes spews out of the machine on a level with your waist, remaining neatly pinned in place, awaiting collection. It all seems too simple to be true. The machine has given you money. This is now your money. Two hundred quid. Just like that. No questions asked. Once again, you glance about you, but no one is paying you the slightest attention. You take the notes, fold them in half, and stick them in the back pocket of your trousers. You begin to press the button to retrieve your bank card, but pause. Perhaps this is something you can do again? Another day; when you need more money? It would be good to know just how much Alfred Wurgihurt is worth.

You study the options more closely. You press a couple of buttons experimentally, but do not get to the screen you want. Someone is now queueing behind you to use the machine, and you are conscious that you are taking a long time; the last thing you want now is for a member of staff to come over to see if there is a problem. You stab a last button, randomly, hopefully. A figure appears on the screen. It is a larger figure than you have ever seen before. It has several noughts at the end of the number, where you are not used to seeing them; more noughts even than amounts you had dealt with in your homeland, where the currency was practically worthless. You think that you must have made a mistake. Can this really be the balance of Alfred Wurgihurt's account? You walk away from the machine, slightly stunned; your head in a daze of figures.

"Oi! Mister."

Fight or flight? You prepare to run. The two hundred quid in your pocket will give fuel to your steps. You don't look back towards the accusing voice. The door of the bank and safety is only a couple of steps and a big green push-button away.

"Oi! Mister. You forgot this."

Standing at the position that you had just vacated by the cash machine is a young man in paint-stained builder's overalls. He is holding out towards you Alfred Wurgihurt's bank card.

"You left it in the machine."

You take the card, avert your gaze, and murmur a few words of thanks, before pressing the big green push-button to freedom.

Chapter Twenty-One

We're Only Making Plans for Alfred

The seasons changed. Spring became summer. The produce of the allotment changed again, too. There were peas and tomatoes. A variety of beans and berries. Broccoli and cauliflowers. A nice crop of new potatoes. Courgettes under the Polytunnels and, in several plots, courgettes grown so unfeasibly large that they looked like strange invaders from an alien world of giants. You ate them, one and all.

You had had several boring admin tasks to deal with. First of which had been paying your annual rent. Now that you were back in funds, you place three of your crisp twenty-pound notes in the same envelope that the demand for rent had first arrived in, rewrote the number of your allotment plot in bold script on the front and, in the dead of night, stuffed the payment underneath the front door of the Allotment Association's communal clubhouse. As far as you were concerned, your debt was now cleared; you had bought yourself another year's leasehold tenancy of a modestly proportioned single-storey property with a south-facing garden in a desirable postcode. You had also been required to do your accounts. Now that you were a wealthy man, you found yourself taking much more notice of your finances than you had previously. It was not a job that you particularly relished, but you were sufficiently self-aware to realise that, on the whole, you preferred your newly acquired rich man's problems to your old ones when you had been living penniless on the streets. One difficulty that has arisen as a result of your new status was the requirement for much more frequent visits to the bank. Daily visits, in fact. Although, you had discovered that you could limit your visits to only once every two days provided that you went there on the stroke of midnight. It was a slightly inconvenient routine, but it is surprising how quickly you can adapt to anything. The reason for this procedure? Well, it had come about like this:

It had taken several days for the full enormity of Alfred Wurgihurt's bank balance to dawn upon you. You kept replaying in your mind that figure that you had seen displayed on the screen of the cashpoint machine. Had you imagined it? Or misread it? Rationally, though, you knew that you had not been mistaken. Figures do not lie. The fact was that you had funds to draw upon beyond those of your wildest dreams. You would want for nothing. You were sitting pretty. In fact, you were sitting so pretty, that that is exactly what you did for quite a number of days after that first, momentous return from the bank. You put your feet up and you sat around the summerhouse in a state of leisurely indolence that only wealthy people can enjoy. You didn't work on the hole beneath the hatch; you rarely went out scavenging for food. There suddenly seemed less point to all the activities, which had kept you so busy beforehand. Why bother grafting for your daily needs when you had all the money in the bank just to purchase them? It required a shock to stir you from this state of inertia and, four days after your return from the bank, it was a shock that you received. Or, rather than a shock, more a dawning enlightenment. Your funds were not limitless. They came with a timeframe attached, and it was a timeframe limited by the expiry date on Alfred Wurgihurt's bank card. There was no cause for immediate panic. The first thing you had done was to check the actual date when the credit card would be rendered void, and it still had just over eighteen months to run. You had done a few calculations. While your maximum cashpoint withdrawals were limited to £200 per day, over a period of eighteen months, you could still withdraw close on £110,000 if you made a visit to the bank every day. It was an amount nothing like the full sum that was in Alfred Wurgihurt's account, but it was a figure not to be sneezed at. But you were going to have to work for it. No more idle lazing; instead, those daily visits across the bridge, to the bank in the promised land; or, those once every two day visits, if you withdrew one lot of £200 out at a minute before midnight and a further £200 at one minute after midnight. Smart planning. Good time management. It all came back to your engineer training.

You now needed a safe place to stow all the cash you were steadily amassing, and the place you hit upon was the cave. Because a cave it was that you discovered beneath the hatch in the shed. A cave of sorts. Although not a natural one; clearly something manmade. You did not know the word 'grotto' but, if you had, that would have been the word you would have used to describe it. Once you had made the initial breakthrough, it had been a relatively quick and easy job to expand the hole in the bricks to such a degree that you could gain access to the space beyond. Initially, you had explored your new realm with the light from your

Maglite, but the extent of the grotto was much larger than you had first imagined, and you had begun to find it frustrating that you could only illuminate one small corner at any one time. As much as anything, the dark corners and unlit expanses made the entire area feel slightly threatening and remote; you were not so rational not to retain something of the child's primitive fear of Bogeymen hiding in the dark. Also, it left the territory feeling unconquered. Whilst the dark held sway, you were still an interloper; only welcome on sufferance.

It was a relatively simple matter—involving a modest outlay from your cash surplus, and a bit of technical know-how—to extend a new cable, which linked to the existing electricity supply in the summerhouse, through the hatch, and into the grotto. At first, you introduced a series of free-standing lights, but it was not long before you replaced them with a string of bulbs running across the ceiling of the entire underground chamber. The lighting threw the space into a completely new relief. You discovered secondary passages, which you had previously overlooked; secret niches and alcoves; in one stone recess, you discovered the complete skeleton of an adult human.

The discovery sounds as though it should have been frightening, but you didn't feel that emotion at all. Instead, you experienced a sense of kinship. Like yourself, here were the bones of a fellow troglodyte from some past generation. How many years ancient? You couldn't begin to guess. The bones were well preserved, although the clothing around them had perished to nothing more than rags. On the floor, beside the skeleton, something bright attracted your attention, reflecting the light of one of the bare, overhead bulbs. It was a large silver ring, which looked as though it had fallen from one of the skeleton's bony fingers. Instinctively, you tossed it up in the air, catching it again, assessing its weight. There were some characters engraved in the surface of the metal; harsh, angular symbols, which looked like part of the Runic alphabet. You took the ring and concealed it in the same hiding place you had selected for your stash of cash. It would be safe there.

You wondered what to do with the skeleton? Should you bury it? Perhaps in the same grave as Alfred Wurgihurt? It would be a big job, but it seemed as though it was the decent thing to do. The earth beneath the cloches could do with a fresh turn in any case.

Then there was the grotto. What to do with that? That was a bigger question and something that would occupy more of your time. You had plenty of plans. Big plans. First you would move your bedroom underground. You had always been conscious of how exposed the *chaise longue* was from the summerhouse window, and it was only good fortune that had prevented you from being spotted on a couple of mornings when you had overslept. If you bought yourself a new self-build bedframe, it would be easy enough to transport through the hatch and construct in situ. A mattress might be more of a problem, but you did not think that it would be an unsurmountable difficulty. You'd need heating, too. You had found the grotto reasonably dry, but it could be cold, and you had yet to experience what it was like living underground during the winter. It would be relatively easy to set up a few portable heaters but, in the long term, it would be good to have something a bit more permanent; a bit more eco-friendly. After that? Well, the sky's the limit? What did rich people have in their fancy basement conversions? A wine cellar, perhaps? A games room? A cinema room? A home gym? Sauna and spa? Perhaps a heated swimming pool? There was room enough for them all and more. Then there was the question of décor. A colour scheme would have to be considered. And furnishings. Some paintings would help to brighten up the walls. Perhaps a statement sculpture. This was all detail, though. What really mattered was that you had finally found somewhere that you could call a home again. A secret subterranean home beyond the door of a humble garden shed in the middle of a quiet west London allotment.

It was the kind of prize that neighbours might kill for.

Chapter Twenty-Two

The Dane, the Englishman, and the Refugee

Four hundred years after Alfred Wurgihurt's sojourn in the summerhouse, in a post-apocalyptic England, a dirty, naked creature, human, but scarcely human, is scrabbling in the earth, close to the big river. The creature uses a jagged shard of metal as a primitive shovel. It is slow work, but the creature toils tirelessly. Some instinct tells it that there is something buried there; something to eat. The first bone it encounters is not encouraging—there is precious little meat to be had there—nevertheless, it continues digging, revealing more bones. Maybe one will have something to gnaw on?

Four hundred years after Alfred Wurgihurt's sojourn in the summerhouse, in a futuristic England, Contract Commission Team Alpha Gamma is excavating land for a new Magno Rail station, close to the river. An initial survey of the soil, indicates the remains of three skeletons all buried in the same site. Quantum DNA analysis reveals one body to be that of a young male of Scandinavian origin, roughly eight hundred years old; the second, the body of an elderly male of part Western European, part Celtic ancestry, dating back approximately four hundred years; and the third, dating from the same period, a middle-aged male, of Middle Eastern ancestry, possibly originating from the Levant. Preliminary toxicology analysis suggests that all three males had died as the result of a simple organic poison.

A small ammonite fossil discovered in the same location was dated as mid-Cambrian period. Cause of death: unknown.

Printed in Great Britain
by Amazon

62921304R00081